Twoey & the Goat

Robbie Timmons

 mitten press

All inquiries should be addressed to:
Mitten Press
An imprint of Ann Arbor Media Group LLC
2500 S. State Street
Ann Arbor, MI 48104

Printed and bound at Edwards Brothers, Ann Arbor, Michigan, USA

10   9   8   7   6   5   4   3   2   1

Library of Congress Cataloging Data on File.

ISBN-13: 978-1-58726-517-4
ISBN-10: 1-58726-517-6

This book is dedicated to best friends...
especially to my husband, Jim Brandstatter,
for his love and support
and for being my best friend.

Contents

PART ONE

To Be a Champion

CHAPTER ONE

A Champion Is Born

The barn was so dark, not even a shadow could be seen. Amy crept inside and carefully, quietly closed the barn door. As she walked in the blackness she heard movement, but she was not afraid. Actually, she felt comforted. She had visited the barn many times every day and knew every inch of it. She could recognize every sound.

Suddenly, she felt something touch her shoulder. She raised her hand and gently stroked Molly's muzzle. The older mare had lived in the barn for a long time and was almost like a grandmother to the thoroughbred mares who also lived there. Many stalls in the barn were filled with little champions the mares had foaled.

Amy felt the tension in the air as she continued to stroke Molly's neck. It was unusual that the thoroughbreds had made no sound when she came into the barn. Amy could tell they were not asleep and she sensed that they were jittery. They knew that something was happening and it wasn't good. That same feeling of dread had awakened Amy in the middle of the night and prompted her to get out of bed and run to the barn.

Molly was relieved to see Amy come into the barn. Molly was experienced in foaling, so she knew that once the doctor and Amy's father came, it would not be long before a new thoroughbred champion would be born. But this time was different. Too much time had passed since the doctor had arrived and the stillness of the stables was now filling with activity.

It was still dark when Amy's mother joined them in the barn. Molly had stuck her head out of her stall so she could enjoy her usual caresses, but Amy's mom ran quickly past, not even looking at her. The barn was filled with human voices. Molly knew that the time had come for Queenie to foal. Yesterday, she had heard Queenie make preparations in her birthing stall. Molly could only wonder what could be taking so long. Why wasn't the foal born yet? The mare saw Amy standing in the light at the end of the barn, waiting with the others.

The other racehorses in their stalls at the J.R. Brand Ranch could sense trouble, too. The thoroughbreds were used to their daily schedule. They loved the pampering and attention. They loved the comfort of a daily routine—their feeding time, grooming, physical examination, exercise, and then the best part of the day—the racing! With their manes and tails flying as their legs stretched and pounded the track to go faster and faster, they proved that they were the best. But, the fear that was now in the air made them feel tense and jittery. In the darkness of the barn, even the racehorses knew something was different about today. One of their friends was in danger.

"Queenie's in bad shape after having such a rough time of it," Dr. Jeremy confided to Amy's mom and dad. "I've done all I can do."

Amy had gotten close enough to hear the vet's words. Her eyes welled up with tears as she understood that her beautiful mare might die. She ran to her mom and buried her face in her arms. Her dad put his arm around them both. They could not reassure Amy that Queenie would live; they could only give her comfort.

Seeing the look of despair on their faces, Dr. Jeremy tried to give them some hope. "Queenie has strong breeding and a strong will. It may be enough to see her through."

As Dr. Jeremy packed up his veterinarian's bag, he added, "I'm sorry we couldn't save the first foal, but I'm hopeful that the second foal will make it. He has champion bloodlines in his favor but, like any foal, he needs a lot of nourishment and love."

Amy looked into the stall and, in the dim light, could see her beloved Queenie lying in the corner. She had to go to her. Amy slowly and quietly went in the stall.

As Dr. Jeremy continued talking with the adults, Amy knelt by Queenie. Amy looked at the mare through tear-filled eyes. As Amy gently stroked Queenie's neck, the mare raised her head. She looked at Amy and gave a small whinny.

Amy smiled. "I love you, too, Queenie. I'll help you get well and, when you're better, we'll go outside to your favorite green pasture. You can gossip with Molly and your other friends." Amy gave Queenie a big hug around the neck and then gently laid Queenie's head on the soft bedding. "You sleep and rest now."

As Amy was getting ready to stand up, she felt a shove from the back that pushed her to her knees. She turned to look into the eyes of the still-wobbly colt. She caught her breath as the newborn foal looked at her. He was beautiful! His big brown eyes were fringed with long black lashes. He tilted his head to study her, and he seemed to be smiling. Her fear about Queenie and sorrow over the loss of the first foal began to lessen as foal number two stared into her eyes and warmed her grieving heart.

"Hey there, Twoey, how ya doin'?" Amy whispered as she

ran her hands over the colt's neck. He nuzzled her cheek as she smoothed her hands over his back and legs. He was small for a thoroughbred colt, but her examination found no abnormalities or apparent problems. Twoey flicked his tail as if to say hello. They looked into each other's eyes again.

Amy smiled at the newborn colt and said, "Twoey. That name fits you just fine, doesn't it?" Twoey nodded his head as if he agreed with her. Amy let out a giggle of surprise as she was convinced Twoey had actually answered her.

Twoey then spotted his mother and gingerly walked on wobbly legs to her side. His eyelids began to droop as he started to fall asleep. Even with his eyes closing, he nuzzled his mother and began nursing.

Amy tiptoed out of the stall and took another look at her beautiful Queenie and her new colt, Twoey. She turned out the light. Amy motioned her mom and dad to the stall door. As they looked in, the stall was quiet and peaceful as the animals slept.

Molly had listened to Amy's tenderness with Queenie and the colt. She thought of the colt's new name and said to herself, "Twoey. What a strange name for a champion racehorse. He'd better get strong fast to overcome the teasing he'll receive over that name!"

While Queenie and Twoey rested, the other thoroughbreds felt the tension ease in the barn and they, too, finally slept.

The sun was up too soon for Amy after the night spent in the barn, but she suddenly felt wide awake as she remembered the excitement overnight. She dressed quickly for school, grabbed some fruit for breakfast, picked up her bookbag, and ran to the barn hoping to spend a couple of minutes with Queenie and Twoey before leaving for school. Her heart warmed and she smiled as mother and colt cuddled side-by-side, fast asleep.

12

The daily routine for the thoroughbred racehorses at J.R. Brand Ranch returned to normal. They soon were busy with their schedule of grooming and examinations. Then, exercising and training. Finally, they'd get to show off their athletic skills on the racetrack. They loved the competition! After cooling down, they returned to their stalls for their evening meal and to rest for the night.

Twoey had slept most of the day, waking up just long enough to nurse. Then, he'd curl up again on the soft bedding next to his mother. He woke with a start when he heard noises. He jumped up on his wobbly legs and leaned against his mother for comfort.

"What's happening?" Twoey fearfully asked.

Queenie was pleased that Twoey was alert and asking questions. She explained the daily routine of the thoroughbreds. "The racehorses are coming home for the night. They've been working at the track all day and are still excited from their racing and the competition."

Twoey was silent for a moment and then he asked his mother, "Will I be a racehorse, too, someday?"

"Yes, of course you will. It's in your blood. Your grandfather, Seattle Slew, was one of the greatest thoroughbreds to race. I was chosen to be your mother because I'm a descendant of Secretariat, another champion thoroughbred."

"I can't wait to get outside and run. I bet I beat them all!" Twoey exclaimed with confidence. Queenie looked at her little son with pride.

"We'll both have to get stronger first, little one, then we'll get to go outside in the sun and graze on green pastures. There you can run as fast as your little legs can go."

Queenie closed her eyes so she could visualize that perfect day—the warmth of the sun on her back while her little son romped over the green grass. Her dreamy thoughts were suddenly interrupted by unkind words coming from the champion filly Dynamite Rita, who had just returned to her stall nearby.

"Queenie, dearie," Dynamite Rita called out in a nasty voice, "heard you had a bad time. Lost one foal and number two colt is small and puny. What will become of you and the runt? It takes money to run a thoroughbred ranch like this, you know. If you can't bring in the money through racing or producing good foals, well, you'd better move out." Rita had always been jealous of Queenie because Queenie was the favorite horse at the farm. Rita wanted to hurt Queenie, hoping she would then become the favorite.

The words hurt Queenie more than the pain of foaling. She felt overpowered by the grief of losing one foal. She felt her legs quiver. She lay down. Queenie knew Rita was being nasty to her, but she feared that the mean words were true. Perhaps she was a failure. Her first colt had been born dead and her second colt was small and weak and still struggling to survive. It was her fault. Queenie looked at Twoey, but she looked more closely than she had before. He was small, yes, but he was well formed with strong legs that would become muscular as he grew and exercised.

Queenie called to her little son, "Twoey, come over here a minute, please." As Twoey walked toward her, she looked straight into his eyes. What she saw in his eyes was like a lightning bolt to her heart. She recognized the look. She had seen it in only one other thoroughbred, a true champion.

"He's more than a survivor," Queenie thought to herself. "He has the look in his eyes that only a champion possesses. His heart is in his eyes and it's the heart of a thoroughbred champion." Queenie relaxed. Her fear eased and for the first time since Twoey's birth, she felt confident that everything was going to be all right. She would do whatever she could to help him reach his destiny. "Come lay next to me, Twoey," Queenie said. "Everything's all right."

Molly had heard the crushing words. She came to Queenie's defense and addressed all the horses that were now in their stalls for the night. "All of you have no idea what Queenie has been through, both physically and emotionally. She needs our support." Several of Queenie's friends agreed and gave her sounds of encouragement.

A timid voice was heard coming from stall number 4. A young pregnant filly, Sarah's Dream, would give birth to her first foal in a week. She was nervous and the talk about Queenie's problems increased her fear. "Queenie, you and the colt will be okay, won't you?" Sarah asked.

"Twoey and I will be just fine," Queenie said with confidence as she smiled at Twoey.

"Twoey!? Did you say his name is Twoey?" The shocked question came from Red Regal, a filly in stall number 6. "What kind of name is that?" she snickered. "I can just hear it now." She changed her voice into the flat, deep monotone of the racing announcer. "And down the stretch they come, Red Regal in the lead, Dynamite Rita one length behind, and bringing up the rear, Twoey."

Horse laughter filled the stalls in the barn. Queenie snuggled beside Twoey, who was too young to understand the ridicule. When the jeers quieted, Molly tried to reassure Queenie that the future would be promising, that Twoey would grow up to be a champion, just like his ancestors. For the first time, Queenie knew in her heart that Molly's prediction would come true.

When Amy came into the barn that evening, all the horses had quieted down. She knew and loved each one, but she had her favorites. She had to admit that Queenie, and now Twoey, filled most of her thoughts and her heart. She had been away from them all day and was really anxious to see them, to reassure herself that they were getting healthier. She could not even think of the possibility she could lose one or both of them.

After saying a quick hello to the other horses, she opened Queenie and Twoey's stall. Twoey immediately opened his eyes and got up to greet her. His movement woke Queenie and she stood and walked over to Amy to get a much-needed hug. Amy was encouraged that mother and colt had made it through their first day with no health problems. She immediately noticed that Twoey was less wobbly when he walked.

Amy let out a big sigh of relief. "Oh, Queenie and Twoey...I love you so much!" She put one arm around Queenie's neck and stroked Twoey's back with her other hand. "You are going to make it. I just know it now." She patted Queenie again and kissed the top of Twoey's head. "You both go back to sleep now. Keep getting stronger and I'll see you tomorrow." As she closed their stall gate, she was smiling from ear to ear.

Before she left the barn, Amy stopped at Sarah's stall to give her encouragement. "You're next, sweet Sarah. Only one more week to go." Sarah munched the apple slices that Amy always brought her. She had come to appreciate Amy's soothing voice and touch.

Amy patted the filly lovingly then walked on to Molly's stall. "You help the new moms out now, okay Molly?" Molly always looked forward to seeing Amy. Molly was on the horse farm before Amy was born, so she watched the little girl grow up from the time she was barely able to walk. Molly was the first horse Amy rode when she was just a little girl.

Molly remembered fondly how Amy had shown absolutely no fear when getting in the saddle on a horse that was three times taller than she was. Molly remembered, too, how she had probably been more afraid that day than Amy—afraid the young child would fall off or something bad would happen and it would be Molly's fault. Molly had never stepped so softly or moved so steadily. And now Amy was a teenager, a young woman, who always remembered to bring Molly's favorite treat—mints!

"See you all later," Amy said as she left the barn.

Queenie tried to fall asleep again, but the nightmare of her lost foal and the ridicule that ended the day haunted her again. Will every day be a challenge, she wondered? Will Twoey suffer because she had not been strong enough to bring two healthy foals into the world? Will she have enough strength to nurture Twoey and teach him how to be a champion thoroughbred? Can she teach him to be gentle with humans and other animals? Can he learn to be kind and yet strong? Will he be a good student and learn from his training? Will he have the confidence to win? Will he have the ability to learn from defeat? She had seen the look of a champion in his eyes. She would help him become the best that he could be.

Queenie laid her head next to Twoey's and dreamed of what he could be.

CHAPTER TWO

Finding a Friend

As the morning sun brought light into the barn, it came to life with the familiar sounds of groomers, handlers, and trainers. Horses were being prepared for a new day of racing.

Twoey awoke, filled with excitement. "I wanna see what's happening, Momma."

"Not yet, Twoey. You're still too young, but someday soon," Queenie reassured him.

When the racehorses had left the barn, Amy came in to see how "the girls," as she called them, were doing. First, she visited Sarah's Dream, reassuring her again that she will be a good mother.

Next, Amy stroked Molly along her neck and head and let Molly nuzzle her shoulder, where she placed some apple slices for her old friend. Amy could hardly wait to get to Queenie's stall to see the new mom and little colt. She wasn't disappointed. Mother stood serenely, while little Twoey nursed.

"You be good today while I'm at school. Tonight, if the doctor approves, I'll bring you a special treat," Amy promised them. Then, with her backpack bouncing at her shoulders, Amy ran out of the barn, humming to herself.

Queenie and Twoey slept most of the day. Their rest was interrupted when Dr. Jeremy came into their stall to give them both a checkup.

"Mother and colt are doing exceptionally well," the vet told Amy's mom and dad. "I think they are both out of the woods now. Keep them on their medication and special feed for another week. I'll check them out again, but I don't think you have a thing to worry about now."

They couldn't wait to tell Amy the news. They knew she had not been sleeping well and had done little else but worry about Queenie and Twoey. When Amy got home from school, they greeted her with big smiles and the good news.

"Are they really going to be all right?" Amy cautiously asked, hoping there would be no "ifs" or "maybes."

"Yes, they are both out of danger," Amy's dad reassured her.

"Great!" Amy called out as she did a quick twirl and headed for the door. "I want to tell them the good news!" She ran off toward the barn.

* * * *

Amy did not have school the next day and she was anxious to spend time with the horses. She opened Queenie's stall door and, instead of going in, waited for Queenie to come out, knowing Twoey would follow his mother. Queenie gave out a whinny of excitement. She knew this meant only one thing. Amy was taking Queenie and Twoey outside to the pasture. While Queenie was full of anticipation, Twoey was cautious and afraid to leave his familiar stall.

As they walked along the open stall doors, Amy explained, "Everybody else is outside enjoying the sunshine, but I waited to bring you out last so you can make a grand entrance befitting a queen and her newborn prince." Amy smiled at the mare and colt she loved so much. "I'm taking you to your own special turnout so you can teach Twoey how to behave in the pasture. Later, he can meet some of the other foals that were born earlier this year."

Once they were inside the pasture, Amy closed and locked the gate. She stood there and took a moment just to enjoy watching Queenie and Twoey. She had a lot of chores to do today, but they could wait a minute. The first day a new colt experiences the pasture is not a moment to be missed! She watched for a time as Queenie led a very timid Twoey through the green grass. Satisfied, Amy put the beautiful scene of mother and colt in her mind and turned away to begin her chores.

"This is the pasture," Queenie explained to Twoey, who was hiding behind her legs, peeking out. He saw so much ground covered with bright green grass. He sniffed the ground, inhaling the sweet odor of the lush grass. Queenie was charmed by Twoey's reaction to his first adventure out of the stall. She lowered her head, as if to whisper a secret in his ear, and said, "Even better than the smell is the taste!"

Twoey looked at her in amazement. "You mean we can eat all this stuff?" He looked out over the huge pasture as if it were one big dinner table.

Queenie laughed. "You'll get filled up, little man. Don't worry about being hungry." Twoey thought the pasture must be the greatest place in all the world! While Queenie wanted to kick up her heels, roll on the ground, and run along the fence, she instead stayed by Twoey to reassure him that he had nothing to fear in the strange surroundings.

She playfully trotted ahead of him, then turned and urged him to follow her. Reluctant at first, Twoey took a couple of tentative steps on the soft, green grass. Then, he began to walk a little faster, until he was romping behind his mother. They played for a while on the warm grass but Queenie tired quickly, still recovering from the difficult birth. She led Twoey over to a shady spot under a tree at the edge of the pasture where she laid down with her young son. They were soon asleep.

Twoey woke with a start! He jumped up to look into the eyes of a hairy monster that was staring at him through the fence! His movement woke Queenie, who was instantly up on her legs, ready to protect him from harm. Twoey hid behind his mother's legs, knowing she would make the monster go away. To Twoey's surprise, she began talking to the monster.

"Hi, Captain Kidd. You gave my little one quite a scare. He's not really shy, but everything is so new to him. It will take him a while to learn about the pasture and all the animals that live here."

Captain Kidd, the goat, continued to stare. "He's small, isn't he? Not much bigger than I am."

"Yes, he is small right now, but he'll grow quickly," Queenie answered.

"What's your name?" Captain Kidd asked Twoey. Twoey could only stare back at the strange animal with the horns and hairy face.

"Go ahead and answer him," Queenie said as she nudged Twoey toward the goat. "Captain Kidd is one of the friendliest animals you'll meet on the farm."

Twoey's voice was barely a whisper as he said, "Twoey."

"Gesundheit," Kidd responded, thinking Twoey had sneezed.

"What?" Twoey asked, in a surprisingly louder voice.

"Didn't you sneeze? I was just saying 'God bless you.' That's what you say when someone sneezes," Kidd explained.

Twoey thought this animal was the strangest thing he had ever seen. How was he supposed to talk to someone who made no sense?

Twoey stared at Kidd and indignantly said, "My name is Twoey! Twoey. Twoey. Twoey. Get it?" Twoey continued to stare at the goat, challenging him to reply. He gave the goat a warning look.

Kidd looked down, thinking, then looked up at Twoey and smiled. "Yeah. Hi, Twoey. I'm Captain Kidd the goat, but you can call me Kidd. Well, see ya around." And with that, the little goat was gone.

Twoey looked up at his mother with disbelief in his eyes. "Well, that was strange! Are there a lot of odd animals on the farm to meet?" Twoey asked, hoping the answer was "no."

"There are many animals on the farm that are different from thoroughbreds, but they are kept in their own sections of the farm, each group separated from the others. It will be rare if you meet any other farm animals," Queenie explained.

Twoey was trying to figure it all out. "Well, if I'm probably not going to meet any other farm animals, why did I meet Kidd?"

Queenie had to laugh. "Just fate, I guess. Captain Kidd showed up on the farm a couple months ago. He's the only animal besides the barn cats who is allowed to roam throughout the farm." Seeing that Twoey was still concerned about Kidd, she assured him, "He would never hurt you. He's just very friendly."

"Is he the only goat on the farm? Doesn't he have a mother, or father, or other goats to play with?" Twoey asked.

"He's the only goat," Queenie answered, appreciating the concern she saw in Twoey's eyes. "He's probably very lonely. Most horses ignore him. Some thoroughbreds think they are royalty on the farm and they refuse to talk to other farm animals."

Twoey thought for a moment, then commented, "I'd sure hate to be alone."

Queenie smiled at him. "You, my little man, will never be alone! But Captain Kidd is a good, kind animal and I hope you'll talk with him whenever you see him in the pasture."

"I guess I will," Twoey said quietly, thinking of the funny

looking goat, and added with a smile, "But you have to admit, he is weird looking!"

"Not everyone can be as handsome as you, my young son," Queenie teased.

Mother and colt walked over to the gate, content with their first day in the pasture.

CHAPTER THREE

The Lessons Begin

Several weeks later, Amy led Queenie and Twoey to a bigger pasture where they could join other mares and foals. Amy wanted to give Twoey a pep talk. She considered this to be Twoey's first day at kindergarten.

"There are lots of other foals in the pasture today, so have fun playing with them. They'll teach you games where you can run and jump."

Twoey kept looking up at her as if he understood every word.

"This is your first day where you can play with foals your own age and you don't have to stay right with your mom. I know you'll have so much fun."

Twoey understood what Amy was saying by her reassuring tone and body language. He was allowed to run all over the pasture—with other foals! Wow!

"Go on, now," she said to Queenie and Twoey. "Have fun."

Amy watched as Queenie and Twoey approached the other mares in the pasture. She couldn't help but notice how proud Queenie looked as she showed off Twoey to the mares. "Well, they're going to be okay now," Amy said to herself as she walked down the lane away from the pasture.

Queenie was pleased to be back in the pasture with Molly

and some of the mares that had gathered together. They were her friends and she had not been with them in a while. They all checked out Twoey, who was hanging his head a little, not knowing how to react as his mother's friends were eyeing him. The mares nodded their approval and began commenting on how cute he was and how well he was doing.

Twoey was uncomfortable being the center of attention. He slowly backed away from the group of horses. Realizing they weren't going to call him to come back, he decided he would explore another area of the pasture. He spotted some foals near his size. They looked like they were having fun as he trotted up to them. They stopped playing and began staring at him. He spoke first, "Hi. I'm Twoey, son of Queenie."

One of the colts came up to him and started sniffing him, checking him out in a horsey way. He said, "I'm Prince Ablaze, the leader." Then the other foals approached him and began introducing themselves. Twoey was trying to remember their names—Chestnut Pride, Tireless Two Socks, Flaming Princess, Snap Dragon.

The last filly came up to Twoey, taking timid steps. In a

shy, soft voice she looked at him and said, "My name is Angel Eyes. Glad to meet you, Twoey."

Twoey felt like he had suddenly lost his voice. It seemed that all the other horses disappeared and he could only see this lovely, shy filly standing in front of him. "Angel Eyes," he repeated, in a half-whisper.

Queenie had been watching Twoey closely. She was concerned with how the other foals would react to him. He was still a bit smaller in size, but he was growing nicely and was healthy. She knew that foals could be mean to each other, especially to one who might be a little different. She admitted to herself that Twoey was different. But to her, he was different in a very special way. She knew from his struggle at birth that he was a fighter and a winner. She also knew that, being a thoroughbred, he would always need that fighting spirit and the drive to win.

Queenie viewed this first meeting with his peers as his first test. It was the first of many challenges he would have to face without her.

Twoey felt like he was hypnotized as he watched Angel

Eyes. He suddenly realized the other foals were talking to him.

"Snap out of it, runt!" Prince Ablaze said to a stunned Twoey. Prince Ablaze looked at the other foals and said, "Come on, let's go. We don't need him to play with us." With that, Prince Ablaze stared at the foals, willing them to follow him. They did.

Twoey lowered his head in embarrassment. He had been so happy to meet new friends. Now they had run away and were laughing and playing without him. Twoey slowly raised his head and, to his pleasant surprise, Angel Eyes was still there.

"Why didn't you leave with the others?" he asked her, with surprise in his voice.

"Well, since this is your first day in this pasture, I thought maybe you needed a tour of the place." Angel smiled. "C'mon, I'll show you around." She turned and pranced away. Twoey quickly and happily followed along behind her.

Twoey and Angel Eyes walked side-by-side. Angel took Twoey to the fence that separated their pasture from other fields where the racehorses were grazing. Twoey looked at them with awe. They were so big and muscular. They held their heads high, as if expecting to wear a crown. They were magnificent.

"Look over there, Twoey. See that black stallion over in the corner by himself? That's Diamond Knight. He's the best thoroughbred at the farm. He's won nearly every race."

Twoey thought the black stallion must be the king of all stallions. His black coat glistened in the sun. He was very tall and muscular. Lost in his own thoughts about Diamond Knight, Twoey suddenly realized that Angel was still talking.

"He just missed winning the Kentucky Derby by a nose. Everybody says it wasn't his fault. Something on the track caused him to stumble. I hear he's pretty angry. No one goes near him. They say he's mean, and he bites, and he doesn't want to be around any of the other horses."

Twoey stared at the huge black stallion. "So that's what a true champion looks like," Twoey said, quietly. He started walking along the fence. "Can we get closer? I sure would like to see him up close."

"No way!" Angel said with alarm. "You stay away from him. He could break every bone in your body."

Twoey couldn't take his eyes off the magnificent black stallion. Angel finally urged him away from the fence. "Now come on, let's go see our moms. It's time to go in."

Angel led the way. Twoey followed, but couldn't resist a glance back at Diamond Knight. He noticed the stallion had stopped grazing and was looking at him.

Twoey's dreams that night were filled with visions of rolling hills, covered with soft green grass, where he and Angel Eyes were laughing and playing. The bright colors of the dream were suddenly covered in black. A huge black stallion with his mane waving in the wind reared up on his hind legs. His head lifted, turning from side-to-side, and he let out a loud cry. Twoey tried to run away, but his legs wouldn't move.

"Twoey. Twoey, wake up. You're dreaming," Queenie urged.

"Oh, Mama. He was right here and he was so big," Twoey cried.

"Well, no one's here and you're okay. It was just a nightmare. See? Everything's as it should be. Now try to get some rest. It will be daylight soon," Queenie reassured him.

Twoey's breathing slowed to normal, but there would be no more sleep tonight.

CHAPTER FOUR

Meeting a Mentor

As the sun filtered into the barn, Amy arrived right on schedule. Twoey had been counting the minutes until she would open the stall door and lead Queenie and Twoey to the pasture again.

"You liked the pasture, didn't you, Twoey?" Amy asked.

Twoey nodded his head, as he always did when he agreed with Amy. It always made her laugh and he liked seeing her smile.

"I'm going to take you to a different pasture today, so you'll have a new place to explore," Amy explained.

While Amy seemed excited about taking them some place new, Twoey was disappointed. In this pasture, Twoey was the only foal. He didn't see Angel Eyes or the other foals anywhere. He could see Molly in the far corner of the pasture, and he watched as his mom galloped away to see her friend.

Twoey decided he would explore this new pasture on his own. There were so many new sights and smells! Twoey spotted a little flower by the fence and was walking over to get a whiff when his left foreleg stepped into a gopher hole. He tumbled down on the ground. "Ouch," he cried out.

"You've got to watch where you're walking. You don't want to break a leg. Your bones aren't very strong yet." The voice was deep and strong and was coming from the other side of the fence.

Twoey looked up into the dark eyes of the black stallion. His first reaction was fear. He felt like he was in the middle of last night's nightmare. He couldn't even stand up.

From the ground, Twoey stared at the huge thoroughbred that was towering over him. He remembered Angel Eyes saying he could break every bone in Twoey's body.

"Are you hurt?" Diamond Knight asked him.

Twoey couldn't speak. He just continued to stare.

"Come on, get up," the stallion urged. "You look like you're okay. Only way to find out is to stand on that leg."

Twoey slowly got up on his forelegs, then his hind legs. He didn't even stand tall enough to reach the top of the stallion's legs. He stretched his neck upward to look into the eyes of Diamond Knight, who was looking down at him.

"You're Diamond Knight, the champion of all thoroughbreds here," Twoey finally managed to say.

"Yes, that's my name. And I guess I am a champion. I've won lots of races, but it takes a lot of work, everyday, to stay a champion," Diamond answered. "Are you going to be a champion, Twoey?"

"You know my name?" Twoey asked incredulously.

The stallion nodded. "Everyone knows the son of Queenie and the story of his fight to survive," the stallion replied. "Now, are you going to be a champion?"

"I want to be," Twoey said quietly, with some hesitation.

Diamond Knight lowered his head over the fence so his flaring nostrils were only inches from Twoey's nose. "Not good enough!" he snorted.

Twoey was shaking.

Diamond Knight ignored Twoey's fear and continued, "You have to want to be a champion so badly that you demand

it of yourself, work every day for it, and know in your heart and your head that you are a champion. You'll train until you're exhausted and hurt all over. Then, you'll demand more of yourself. You'll never stop because when you stop training and demanding, you stop winning. Can you do that? Do you want to do that?" Diamond demanded.

Twoey didn't know what to say. He could feel Diamond's breath in his face and see the stallion's dark eyes peering into his eyes and into his heart and soul. He remained speechless.

Diamond lifted his head a little and gave a small laugh. "Think about what I said, Twoey. It takes total dedication to become a champion. I hope you'll accept the challenge when you're ready. You have the heart of a thoroughbred, you know. It's in your eyes and in your breeding. That means it's in you to do your best and then give more than your best, until you've given it all away."

Diamond's tone was softer this time and Twoey was regaining his courage. "You don't seem mean at all," Twoey finally said, then wished he hadn't said it.

Diamond chuckled. "The weak ones are afraid of me and the strong ones stay away to avoid confrontation, so I pretty much rule the farm."

"But don't you miss having friends?" Twoey wondered.

"I used to have a lot of friends. But it's hard keeping friendships at the racetrack." Diamond looked out over the pasture, as if remembering. "Every time I beat some of my friends, I felt badly, but that's what I was trained to do. I wanted to be the best and I worked hard to achieve it. It was my destiny to be a champion."

Diamond's thoughts returned to the present. "Now, I find it's easier to be alone because I can't stand to see the look of defeat on the faces of my friends and know I'm the one responsible for it. Because of my determination to win, many of my friends have been sent away from here to race in other places. I doubt I'll ever see them again. I don't even know what happened to them."

Diamond looked back at Twoey with sadness in his eyes. "There are many sacrifices involved in being the best. But, if that's your destiny and your heart's desire, sacrifice becomes part of your life. There are also many joys in being a champion. You have to embrace the joy and accept the sacrifice required to meet your goal."

Diamond smiled at Twoey and started to walk away. "I've talked enough. Better be going. Glad you're okay."

Twoey's fear of Diamond had disappeared. The fear had changed to admiration and respect. Twoey saw several things in Diamond's eyes—confidence, control, a look of caring and concern—but also a glint of sorrow.

As Diamond walked away, Twoey asked, "Will you help me, Diamond? Will you help me to be a champion?"

Diamond stopped and turned to look at the little foal.

Twoey went on, "I really want to be a champion like you, and I promise I'll work hard. The other colts say I'm too small to be a champion." Twoey dropped his head a little. "They don't like me," he admitted. "They make fun of me because I'm smaller and I don't have a fancy name."

Diamond took a few steps toward Twoey and said, "Look at me, Twoey." Twoey did as commanded. Diamond looked deep into Twoey's eyes and heart and said, "You have a special destiny. Don't worry about your size. Your growth will come. Your father is very tall, as is your mother. As for your name, it's up to you to make it represent whatever you want. Do you want the name "Twoey" called out as winner, time and time again? Do you want the name "Twoey" to go into the record books as one of the best thoroughbreds at this farm, perhaps in the world?"

Twoey could imagine it. His eyes sparkled as he thought of his name being announced as a winner. He imagined the pride he would feel and how his mother could brag. The others wouldn't make fun of him then. As if awakening from a dream, Twoey looked straight at Diamond Knight and answered, "Yes, I do want it."

"Then start today. Be the champion in your mind. Keep your eyes focused on your goal. And strengthen your heart to withstand the physical and mental preparation so you won't be tempted to quit when it becomes difficult."

"I feel like I could do anything and be anybody when I'm with you," Twoey said with admiration.

"It's in *you* to be whatever you want to be. I can't do it for you," Diamond said.

Then he smiled and added, "But I'll keep an eye on you to make sure that when you stumble and fall, you'll get up and learn from your mistakes." With that, Diamond trotted off to the shady corner of his pasture.

Twoey stood at the fence for a while watching Diamond Knight, making sure it wasn't a dream. He couldn't believe he had actually been talking to the champion racehorse. As he was replaying the conversation in his mind, he was suddenly struck from behind and fell to the ground. Looking around angrily, Twoey shouted, "What was that for?"

The little gray-and-white goat stared at him as if he were out of his mind and yelled, "Are you CRAZY? Do you know who that is? Diamond Knight, the horse of fright!"

Twoey stared back at Kidd while he got back up on his legs. "No, you're the crazy one!" he yelled back. "He's not the horse of fright. In fact, he didn't scare me at all," Twoey added with a smug look.

The goat laughed. "Oh, yes, he did. I saw your legs shaking."

"Well, only at first," Twoey admitted with a grin. "He's actually pretty great. I like him. He has his reasons for not being friendly to some of the other horses," Twoey explained, then added with pride, "He and I are going to be friends."

"Now I KNOW you're crazy. Why would he want to be friends with a little colt, and why YOU?" The goat laughed again.

"Well," Twoey said, hesitating and thinking. It did sound crazy. "We have a lot in common."

Kidd was speechless. He dropped his head and shook with laughter.

Twoey continued, trying to say the words with the same kind of confidence he saw in Diamond Knight. "He thinks I can be a champion, and I do, too."

The goat's laughter got louder and boomed over the pasture.

Twoey was getting angry. He decided he had enough of Kidd's laughter! He started walking toward Kidd with his head lowered and ears back in a threatening manner.

Twoey angrily shouted, "Listen, you four-legged, hairy, horned beast, I WILL be a champion. I'll prove it to you and to everybody who makes fun of me. I don't care if you and the others laugh at me. Go ahead and laugh now because you won't be laughing when I prove myself on the racetrack." With that, Twoey gave the goat a nudge with his head. "Go on, get away from me."

Kidd didn't budge and looked at Twoey with new understanding. He said, "You know, you and I have more in common than I thought. Nobody likes me either. They all tell me to get away from them." Kidd lifted his head and pretended to prance like a thoroughbred. "They're too good to be seen with me. After all, they are mighty thoroughbreds and I'm just a goat." Kidd lowered his head in sadness.

Twoey suddenly found the whole situation funny and began to laugh. "What a pair we are," Twoey chuckled. "A couple of misfits."

The goat smiled back at him and said, "Yeah, that's us."

Kidd the goat looked between the fence boards into the next pasture, taking a good look at Diamond Knight, the magnificent, champion black stallion. He turned back to Twoey. "Well, I'll say one thing for you, Twoey, you sure know how to pick 'em!"

Kidd moved to stand beside Twoey and offered a truce. "Look, if you want to be friends with Diamond Knight, that's up to you. But why not be friends with somebody your own size? Like me, for example?"

"I'll think about it if you promise not to butt into me again," Twoey responded.

"But that's what I do," Kidd said, laughing. "I butt things. It's fun. That's why I have these little horns."

Twoey did not see the logic or pleasure in it. He snapped back, "Well, I don't think it's fun, and I don't appreciate your making me the butt of your joke."

"The butt of my joke?" Kidd giggled. "You have quite a horse sense of humor."

When Twoey looked as if he still didn't see what was funny, Kidd impatiently explained. "I butt things. You don't want to be the butt of my joke. Get it?" With that, the goat broke out into all-out laughter, pleased with his own little joke.

Twoey couldn't sort out his emotions. He felt angry at the goat, humiliated that he'd been knocked down and laughed at, but some little tickle inside him made him want to laugh.

Kidd noticed Twoey's discomfort and said, "Look, I don't want to hurt you. I just want someone to play with. How about it?"

Twoey thought about it for a minute. "Yeah, okay." He decided it would be fun to have Kidd as a friend.

Twoey and Kidd took off running, jumping, and kicking around the pasture.

Queenie had been keeping her eye on Twoey while she talked with Molly. "Looks like Twoey has found a buddy," Molly said with a smile to Queenie.

"When they said 'opposites attract,' I doubt they had a thoroughbred colt and a goat in mind," Queenie answered, while watching the two chase each other around the pasture. "Most youngsters don't judge. They see the fun in someone else, not the difference between them. I hope Twoey never loses that quality."

As the sun began to set, the thoroughbreds were led out of the pastures and into their stalls for the night. Twoey wanted to stay outside just a little longer so he tried to be the last one to leave the pasture. When he got back into his familiar stall, his whole body felt tired. The soft bedding tempted him to lie down and he was soon sound asleep.

His dreams were filled with images of a funny little furry head with small horns on top and the sounds of his own laughter as he and his new friend played in the pasture. In the distance, watching over them, he saw the shadow of a black stallion.

CHAPTER FIVE

Double Trouble

Twoey was awakened by the now-familiar morning sounds of the racehorses being prepared for another day. Twoey was anxious to go to the pasture again, anxious to begin what he knew would be a day filled with adventure. He might get to talk with Diamond Knight again. He might get to play with Kidd. Twoey whinnied at the thought he might get to see Angel Eyes again. He hoped Amy would come early to let him out of his stall today. There was so much to see and do in the pasture and he needed to get an early start.

When Amy came by with her daily treats for Twoey and Queenie, Twoey decided to let her know he wanted out. He kicked his back legs, ran around in circles, and made as loud a whinny as he could. It was a real temper tantrum.

"Well, look at you," Amy said to him. "Feeling a little frisky, are you? Okay, come on, I'll take you and your mom to the pasture." Amy was so happy to see the progress Queenie and Twoey were making. Queenie was nearly back to complete health and Twoey was growing, filling out, and gaining muscle strength. Amy hoped that her tender loving care had a lot to do with their recovery.

As Amy opened the stall door, Twoey felt very pleased with himself for making Amy take him to the pasture this early in the day. Queenie, however, was not happy with his behavior. Twoey had learned an effective, but bad, lesson—if he acted up, he got his way.

Queenie and Twoey were taken by Amy to the same pasture as yesterday, the one where Twoey had talked with Diamond Knight over the fence and played with Kidd the goat. Amy knew she no longer had to keep such a close watch over Twoey or Queenie. So, after she led them inside the pasture, she closed the gate and left to do her chores.

Twoey saw a group of foals across the pasture, and he looked to see if Angel Eyes was with them. He didn't see her or her mom, Sarah's Dream. He glanced across the fence into Diamond Knight's pasture, but he didn't see the stallion either.

"Darn," Twoey complained to himself. "The only ones in the pasture are the foals who laughed at me." He didn't have anybody to play and romp with. Twoey decided to hang back with his mom for a while.

Queenie was talking to Molly the mare about the new foal just born to Sassy Dancer. "She's so cute," Queenie said.

"And, she stood right up and began nursing just moments after being born," Molly added.

Twoey had heard enough of the newborn foal talk. He was bored but did not want to go over near the other foals that had rejected him. Just then, he heard a whisper from the other side of the fence.

"Come on, let's get out of this pasture. I've got something to show you." It was Kidd.

"But I can't get out of the pasture," Twoey sighed with disappointment. "Maybe you can crawl under the fence but I can't, and the gate is closed."

"Oh, I know how to get it open! Stand back." And with that, Kidd stretched up on his hind legs, lifted the gate latch with his head, and pushed the gate open.

Twoey looked back to make sure his mother was busy talking to Molly, and then he slid through the open gate to follow Kidd.

"I think it's about time you had a tour of the whole farm," Kidd said to Twoey as they walked away from the pasture.

Kidd led Twoey past several barns. They stood hidden behind one barn and peered around it to see an area filled with equipment and horses.

"This is where some of the horses come to exercise. Over there, they are hooked up to those poles and then they follow each other around in circles."

"That looks more like work than fun," Twoey observed.

"If you want to see the real fun," Kidd exclaimed, "then follow me." Kidd took the lead down the road behind the barns and then turned into some trees. "We have to be careful we're not seen over here," Kidd explained with excitement. "We'd get in really big trouble."

Twoey looked out through the trees to see a huge fenced-in track. He noticed it wasn't a circle, but was straight for a while, then curved, then straight again, then another curve.

"What's this?" Twoey asked.

"This is a real oval racetrack where all the horses practice running and they try to beat the other horses. The horse that runs faster than all the others receives lots of attention and gets treats."

"What about the horses that don't run the fastest?" Twoey asked with concern.

"Oh, they get attention, too, but sometimes they get scolded for not running fast. Then, they get another chance. Maybe the next time they will be the fastest."

Twoey looked at the track with yearning in his eyes. "Look!" Twoey exclaimed, "there's Diamond Knight!"

The black stallion looked regal. He was in total control as

he raced around the track, appearing as if he was just taking his jockey along for the ride. He ran easily, and Twoey sensed he could run twice as fast if he wanted. He wasn't competing. It was not a race. It was more of an exercise. Twoey bet Diamond had done it hundreds of times.

Even though it wasn't a real race, Twoey could see the champion spirit in every stride. More now than ever, Twoey was in awe of Diamond Knight.

"Just look at him," Twoey finally said to Kidd. "He's everything I want to be."

"Well, at least you have a shot at it," Kidd complained. "There's no way racing is in my future."

"I'll be the fastest, just you wait and see. And, you can come with me, Kidd, and watch as I leave all the other horses in my dust."

The two friends looked out over the track with big dreams in their heads. Suddenly, those dreams were interrupted by human shouts. "There he is! He's in those trees over there by the racetrack."

"See ya!" Kidd yelled as he took off running as fast as he could to escape. "Good luck," he added, disappearing into the trees.

Twoey was led back to the pasture by the humans who now carefully latched the gate. His mother came running over to him.

"Oh, Twoey, I was so worried when I saw the pasture gate open and you were gone. I thought I'd never see you again. There are dangers you don't know about. Things you are too young to recognize as danger," Queenie warned. Twoey listened with his head down.

"Sorry, Mom," Twoey said, glancing up at his mother. However, the excitement of seeing the farm and Diamond Knight running on the track was stronger than his remorse.

"Mom, you should have seen Diamond Knight running on the racetrack. It was awesome!" Twoey went on to describe all the new things he'd seen.

She listened to him and smiled. She began thinking back to the time in her youth when every sight and sound was fresh and new. All those sights, sounds, and experiences had become so familiar she had forgotten how exciting new adventures could be.

"When will I begin my training as a racehorse, Mom?" Twoey asked breathlessly. Twoey wished he were older, taller, and training to be a racehorse right now.

"Patience," his mother said. "You'll be grown-up and put to work soon enough. Enjoy these playful summer days in the pasture as long as you can. Someday, you'll look back with yearning on these carefree days when we were together."

Queenie wished she could tell her son what was ahead of him. While he looked to the future with confidence and anticipation, she knew the day was approaching when they would be separated forever. Soon, he would leave to live with the other colts.

She had little time left and so much to teach him. She wouldn't be there to protect him. He would have to stand up for himself when confronted by another colt. If he backed down once, the others would pick on him always. She knew if Twoey didn't have confidence in himself with the herd, he would not have confidence to win on the track. If he didn't win, he probably would be sold to race in lower-class races.

No time could be wasted. When Twoey fell asleep in their stall that night, Queenie began planning his schooling. It would begin tomorrow.

While Queenie was planning Twoey's education, Twoey was dreaming. He was trying to run, but his legs just wouldn't go fast enough. He seemed to feel the wind as he ran around the racetrack, and he saw the huge black shadow of a stallion running in front of him. He kept trying to catch the other horse, but he couldn't run fast enough. He ran, not wanting to give up, even though he was getting so tired—so tired. And then, he finally slept without dreaming.

CHAPTER SIX

Leading the Herd

Just after dawn, Amy led Queenie and Twoey to the pasture. They watched some other mares arriving in a pasture next to them.

"Watch out for Stormy Pride," Amy cautioned Queenie. "She's in a bad mood today and might try to bite Twoey."

Queenie had a confrontation with Stormy Pride before, and she knew the mare could be aggressive and mean.

"I don't know what gets into her sometimes," Amy continued. "She acts like she's jealous or something. Anyway, you'll be okay if you stay away from the fence." Amy stroked Queenie's neck as she let the mare go. "I sure am glad you're always in a good mood, Queenie. I know I can depend on you being happy."

As Amy left the pasture, Queenie began Twoey's lessons about horse life. She warned Twoey to stay away from the last mare brought in, Stormy Pride, because she was the most dominant mare in the herd. Twoey was learning his first lesson about each horse's place in the herd and how certain horses had a higher rank over others and became leaders.

Queenie explained, "The dominant horse demands that the herd obey and follow it." Twoey watched Stormy Pride as the mare led the other horses around her pasture. "In the wild, a horse that does not obey the dominant horse will be turned away from the herd and will be left alone. That is not only a horrible punishment for horses, but also a dangerous one. Horses enjoy the companionship of being in a herd, but they also need the protection of a herd."

Twoey learned that when he got older and lived with the male horses he would need to discover who was the leader—the dominant male. He would then have to choose either to follow him and let him be the leader or fight him, if Twoey wanted to become the leader.

Twoey saw the other foals across the pasture, running and playing. He wondered why they didn't have to spend time with their mothers learning horse lessons. Then, he saw Angel Eyes.

"Mom, can I go play with the other foals now? Have I learned enough for today? Please?" Twoey begged.

"Go ahead, Twoey. Have fun," she called out to him as he galloped away.

"Be careful," she quietly said to herself. Queenie knew that if he got into trouble or challenges with the other foals, she would have to stay away and let him handle it himself. It was the only way he would learn.

Twoey worked on building up his confidence as he trotted over to the foals. He especially needed confidence to approach Prince Ablaze, who had laughed at him when they first met. He remembered what Diamond Knight had told him: "Be the champion in your mind." He kept repeating the phrase over and over.

As Twoey approached the group of foals, he said hello to each of them and then asked if they wanted to play a game. It was a game that Kidd had taught him. "It's called chase the rabbit. There's really no rabbit, but you pretend to chase one. C'mon, follow me."

Twoey led the group of foals around the pasture as they

trotted, then galloped—pretending to chase a rabbit. The foals jumped over imaginary fences, and then they would stop to lie down and roll on their backs in the grass, kicking their legs in the air. The pasture was filled with the sounds of happy foals that were whinnying and frolicking.

Prince Ablaze, Chestnut Pride, Tireless Two Socks, Flaming Princess, Snap Dragon, and Angel Eyes all played the game, with Twoey in the lead, until the sun began to set and it was time to leave the pasture. Twoey was so pleased that not only had the foals accepted him, but they accepted him as a leader. He felt as if he had jumped over a huge hurdle in his path toward becoming a champion. Twoey turned to leave. Angel Eyes had not run away with the other foals, but walked quietly beside him. All the foals and mares headed to the horse barn for their evening meal.

Twoey was excited as he told his mom about the foals following him and how it made him feel. "We really had fun together, Mom. They didn't laugh at me this time. We all laughed together."

Queenie was proud that Twoey took the lead. She knew it was a good lesson about growing up and surviving in the herd. He was learning what the other horses would expect of him. There was so much yet to teach him about horses, humans, training, racing, who to trust, and how to succeed. There was so much more she wanted him to know.

She watched Twoey as he got settled on the soft bedding in the stall. In minutes, his eyes were closed.

In his mind, Twoey saw a foal slowly jumping over a little fence. Then, another foal and another fence. Suddenly there were lots of foals jumping over lots of fences. He saw himself watching them—counting them. Then he slept.

CHAPTER SEVEN

Growing Up

The days passed into weeks, the weeks into months. Every day in the pasture, Twoey got a lesson in horse life and what humans expected of him. To Queenie, it seemed all too soon that Twoey had grown up. He was now six months old and as tall as the other colts born in the early spring.

On this cool autumn morning, instead of Amy, one of the trainers came to Queenie and Twoey's stall to lead them out to pasture. They were taken to a new pasture, one Twoey had never seen. His excitement increased. So many new sights and smells to explore. He saw some of his colt friends. They were prancing, kicking, and smelling the new pasture. Twoey ran over to join them.

While Twoey was busy exploring with his pals, the trainer quietly led Queenie out of the pasture. Queenie glanced over her shoulder to see Twoey laughing and playing. He didn't see her leave. Queenie was led to a pasture far away on the backside of the farm.

She thought her heart would break. She felt it was too soon to separate from Twoey. She still had more to teach him. But more than that, she yearned to nuzzle him and tell him she loved him. She worried about how he would handle the separation and knew he would be as lonely as she was.

Queenie couldn't help herself when she whinnied as loudly

as she could for him. "Twoey. Twoey." She was hoping he would hear her and come running to her for just one more day together.

Amy was outside the barn but she could still hear Queenie. Tears ran down her cheeks as she listened to her cries for her foal. Queenie had been placed in the far pasture so Twoey couldn't hear her. This was how it was done on the farm. The day of separation—foal from mother.

All the colts and fillies were being separated from their mothers. Amy heard the frantic calls from the other mothers who had also been taken to back pastures. She couldn't listen anymore and ran to the house to try to shut out the panic and sadness in their cries. Soon she knew she would hear the frightened calls from the foals when they couldn't find their mothers. Amy dreaded this day.

She had been with Queenie and Twoey every day since his birth. She had watched him grow not only in size but also in stature among the other foals. She had watched Queenie teach Twoey how to take his place among the herd. This was separation day. Twoey would never again live with Queenie. This was the day he would have to grow up.

The colts would now live in a new barn, away from the fillies that would have their own home. And tonight, each foal would have to experience the loneliest night of its life, its first night alone in a strange stall.

Amy knew from experience that the young horses would cry for their mothers all night. It was so hard, yet she realized it had to be done. It was part of the growing experience of each foal. Amy covered her ears and wept. She tried to think ahead to tomorrow night, when each foal would accept its separation from its mother and be ready to begin its own journey to become a thoroughbred racehorse.

In the pasture, Twoey and his friends had romped and

chased each other, playing and rolling in the new grass until they had run out of games. Twoey looked across the pasture to locate his mother. He couldn't see her and he thought she must be behind a clump of trees. He decided to go find her and tell her about the new games they had been playing.

He searched everywhere but she wasn't in the pasture. He then noticed none of the other mares were in the pasture either. Some of the colts began calling out for their mothers, running around the pasture trying to find them. Twoey felt a panic in his chest.

Where was she? He was so frightened he could not even move or call out for her.

Then Twoey remembered one of his mother's lessons. Queenie had told him never to panic and not to show fear. She had told him there was nothing he would face that he could not endure. But she couldn't have meant this! How could he conquer the fear, the panic, the heartbreak he was feeling now without her?

He had to think. She had said he must remain calm in order to determine exactly what he was facing because fear would prevent him from finding solutions. She had said the more he learned about a problem or a challenge, the less he would fear it. But Twoey was still afraid. He wanted his mother. He wanted to cry. He wanted to hide.

Then he remembered his mother telling him that the way to overcome fear was to face it, not to hide from it. Why couldn't he remember more of what she tried to teach him? Why hadn't he paid closer attention? What else had she told him?

Then, he remembered. She had said, "Be strong, not only physically, but mentally. You can overcome anything you fear, so there's nothing to fear. If someday I am not by your side, remember I will always be in your heart, and you will be in mine."

Twoey then realized what was happening. He remembered how he had been so anxious to grow up, and yet this day of separation arrived too soon. He knew now he would not live with his mother any longer.

It was his first step toward becoming a mature thoroughbred, but inside he felt like a frightened little foal. "You will always be in my heart, Momma," Twoey whispered. "And I will be in your heart. I'll try my best to make you proud of me. I'll do what you taught me and I'll be the best I can be." Twoey lifted his head, and with determination in his eyes, he decided it was time he became a leader, as his mother taught him. He would lead right now.

As the other colts ran around the pasture in a panic, crying for their mothers, Twoey called them over to him. When they approached him with their heads down in grief and fear, Twoey explained that their mothers had not abandoned them and loved them as much as ever. He told them about the changes that would be taking place, as his mother had told him. He hoped to get them focused on the future.

"Think about the yearling show in a few months," Twoey said. "It will be our first chance to be in the spotlight. After that, it won't be long before our real training begins. This is our first step to becoming a thoroughbred racehorse." By helping the other colts overcome their fear, Twoey felt better, too.

The colts were soon led out of the pasture into a new barn and each was placed in his own stall. When his stall door was latched and the sun set, Twoey felt the sadness begin to suffocate him. He thought he'd never get through the night. The loneliness was overwhelming. Twoey could hear some of the other colts crying for their mothers.

Twoey knew he could not sleep this night. He silently said his mother's name, as it brought him comfort. He tried to remember all the fun things they did together and it made him smile.

Twoey's thoughts were interrupted by a noise at his stall door. He walked over and looked out. He saw nothing to the left, nothing to the right, and was about to turn away when he heard a gruff little voice say, "Hey, look down here!"

"Kidd, is it really you? How did you find me?" Twoey happily said to his friend.

"Believe me, it wasn't easy. I've been walking all over this place, going from barn to barn, stall to stall. I'm tired and hungry," Kidd complained.

Twoey was so relieved to see Kidd that he was afraid he would begin crying in front of his friend. So Twoey decided to yell at him instead. "Well, if it was so much trouble, why did you bother?" Twoey angrily snapped back.

Kidd knew his friend was having a hard time in this first night's separation from his mother. He wanted to help Twoey, but didn't want Twoey to know he was helping him.

"I wanted to check out your new digs. Make sure you had plenty of grub and a nice bed," Kidd replied.

"Yeah, I guess it's okay," Twoey said rather quietly as he looked around his stall, noticing everything for the first time.

"You got any extra food you can throw my way?" Kidd asked. "I'm starving."

Twoey hadn't eaten since he arrived in the stall, so there was plenty of food. He gently grabbed a mouthful of hay and dropped it on the barn floor outside his stall.

"Thanks, buddy," Kidd said with his mouth full. "You know, it's a pretty nice place here. I think I'll eat this little snack and then just bed down for the night right here in front of your stall. That okay with you, Twoey?"

Twoey was filled with emotion to realize that his friend

came to keep him from being lonely. He found it difficult to talk without showing how sad he was, yet he was grateful for Kidd's company. He finally managed to say in an "I-don't-care" tone, "Yeah, Kidd, it's okay with me if you want to sleep there."

"Thanks," Kidd said.

Quietly, Twoey replied, "Thank you, Kidd. Thank you very much." As he said it, Twoey had no idea how quickly his life would be changing.

CHAPTER EIGHT

Time to Train

Amy came to Twoey's stall one morning and proudly showed him an important-looking paper. She held the paper up for him to see as she said, "You're officially a registered thorough-bred racehorse, Twoey. Congratulations."

Of course Twoey had *always* thought he was a thorough-bred racehorse, so he didn't know why Amy was so thrilled about a piece of paper. However, he didn't want to spoil Amy's excitement so he nodded in happy agreement.

She went on to explain what was on the paper. "See here? It says you are a full-blooded thoroughbred, son of Queenie. With this paper, Twoey, you are eligible to compete with other thoroughbred racehorses on the track." She looked him straight in the eye and promised, "I know you can be a great thoroughbred. I've seen you fight to survive and work to become a strong leader. I'll make sure you get the best train-ing. You have the smarts and I know you have the heart."

Twoey now felt Amy's excitement and wanted to start competing right away. He wanted to show her that he could be the best.

Amy saw the flicker of understanding and determination in Twoey's eyes. The intensity in his eyes gave her a little jolt and made her take a step away from him as the true realiza-tion of what she said had filled her heart. "You really *can* be a champion, can't you, Twoey? And you know it!" The fact that this could be a reality and not just a dream sent chills through Amy. She turned and winked at Twoey as if they shared a secret and walked out of the barn, humming a tune and holding Twoey's registration paper tightly in her hand.

Twoey thought of his mom and couldn't resist sending a message her way. "How about that, Mom? I'm a registered thoroughbred. Amy said I have the heart to be a champion. And with you in my heart, how can I lose?" Twoey hoped his mom could somehow hear his thoughts.

Kidd came to the stall as he did every night and noticed Twoey's mood. He looked up at Twoey and asked, "What's up?"

Twoey stood straight and proud and lifted his head as if posing for a picture. "I'm official," Twoey responded with pride.

"You're a fish, what?" Kidd asked, as if he didn't understand what he had heard.

Twoey relaxed and looked down at his friend, laughing. "Not fish...OH-FFI-CIAL thoroughbred racehorse. My racing pedigree papers came in today. I can actually begin racing," Twoey explained.

Kidd saw the pride in Twoey's eyes but couldn't resist giving him a jab. "You thoroughbreds. I just don't understand you. You are born a thoroughbred racehorse, but you have to have a paper telling you you're a thoroughbred racehorse? I was born a goat, I'm still a goat, and always will be a goat—with or without a paper."

Twoey laughed. "What *you* will always be is *funny*. C'mon over, I saved you some food."

* * * *

Twoey still enjoyed short daily romps in the pasture with the other colts—Prince Ablaze, Chestnut Pride, and Snap

Dragon—and, of course, Kidd. But the play was getting shorter and the work longer.

They were led by their halters around in a circle by the trainers and had to obey commands like stop, walk, and follow. The training seemed easy enough but it was becoming constant and Twoey was glad to get back to his stall at night to rest.

Every night Amy would come to his stall. She would talk about her day at school, and Twoey felt like he really knew what she was talking about. In a way, he was in school all day, too—just like Amy. He loved the visits. When she would tell him how well he was doing and how proud the trainers were of his progress, it gave him courage to work through the training even when he felt so tired he didn't think he wanted to take another step.

Kidd also came to the stall every night. He filled Twoey's head with visions of his daily adventures around the farm. He never failed to complain that Twoey was missing out on all the fun because he was training so hard. He always asked if Twoey could just take tomorrow off and come play with him, even though he and Twoey both knew that Twoey had set a goal for himself and would not skip a day of training, even if it was tempting.

Twoey thought the training was actually easy so far, but some of his friends, such as Prince Ablaze, didn't like to be told what to do and sometimes refused. Many nights, as he was being led back to his stall, he would see Prince Ablaze still going through the training, still resisting. The trainers would make him work even longer, trying to force him to do the training drills.

Twoey tried to talk to Prince Ablaze and encourage him to do what the trainers asked. He tried to convince him it would get easier as he completed each training session, but

Prince Ablaze stubbornly refused. He told Twoey he hated the training and that he never wanted to race anyway, so he didn't see why he should train to race.

On New Year's Day, there were no training sessions. Amy came to Twoey's stall carrying a special treat. Giving a little bow, she presented him with a gift. "Congratulations, Twoey. You're officially one year old today—a yearling. Here's your birthday cake."

Twoey saw his favorite treat—carrots. They were formed in a round shape and stacked high. He wasn't sure what a birthday cake was, or even a birthday, but if it meant carrots, he was all for it.

Kidd was nearby, of course, and came running through the open stall gate to see what Amy had brought. Amy reached down and patted Kidd's head as she told him, "Let's make it your birthday, too. Here's a carrot cake for you." Kidd did not wait for an explanation. He didn't need one. He only needed to know that there was a special treat for him. Kidd started nibbling on his carrot cake as soon as Amy began to lower it to the ground. He ate so fast that he hardly took time to breathe.

Twoey laughed as he watched Kidd devour his little carrot cake. Twoey enjoyed the hugs, pats, and caresses Amy gave him before he ate a bite of his carrot cake. He made her laugh when he nibbled at the back of her jacket as she turned to leave.

He was so content. He looked around his stall—his home. He knew Amy loved him, and he was fortunate to enjoy the companionship of his best friend, Kidd, even though Kidd was too busy eating now to be much company. Twoey's train-ers took pride in him and he was getting stronger and bigger. He still missed his mom sometimes, but he had only to look in his heart and she was always right there.

Twoey learned that all thoroughbreds born during the year were officially one year old on January 1, but it didn't lessen his feeling of being special.

CHAPTER NINE

The Show Ring

On a cool morning, Twoey awoke to a feeling of tension in the barn. Amy arrived at his stall and told him that he would be taking his first ride in a horse van. While she was leading him out, she said, "You'll have the chance to show off your training in front of a crowd of people." Amy seemed excited about it, so Twoey decided this would be something especially fun to do.

Kidd had been sleeping in front of Twoey's stall in the place he had claimed as his home since the night that Twoey was separated from his mother. Kidd, too, sensed there was something special about the day.

As Amy led Twoey out of his stall, instead of talking to him calmly as she usually did, she explained excitedly what they would be doing.

Kidd realized quickly that today would be anything but routine. He was always up for a new adventure and he didn't want to miss out on this one. He quietly followed Twoey and Amy.

When Twoey finally saw the big horse van, he didn't want to go inside. His natural instinct to run away when sensing danger or fear took control of him. Twoey was looking for any place to run! He began backing away and he threw his head back, trying to break free of Amy's hold.

But Amy had a firm grip on his bridle. She had anticipated Twoey's fear of the horse trailer. She talked to him softly, soothing him, trying to convince him that it would be a great adventure. As she stroked his neck, she whispered to him, "All you have to do is step inside the van."

Twoey trusted Amy. He knew that she loved him and would not do anything to hurt him. He tried to keep that thought in his mind to push away his fear. He pawed at the ground. He whinnied. He stared at the trailer as if trying to show it that he, Twoey, was in charge. If the trailer had been a horse, he thought surely the horse would have turned and run away, frightened of him. He let his head fall again and his courage fell with it.

Kidd had been watching Twoey. He could see that Twoey was afraid of the horse trailer. He saw Twoey trying to overcome his fear, and he also saw defeat in the horse's body as he dropped his head. Kidd ran as fast as he could, right past Twoey, and jumped into the horse trailer.

"C'mon, Twoey, there's nothing to this," Kidd said as he turned around and looked at Twoey. "See? If a little guy like me isn't afraid, a big, bad thoroughbred like you has nothing to fear."

Twoey's head snapped up and he stared at Kidd in disbelief.

Amy could only smile at Kidd and turn to Twoey, as if leaving the decision up to him.

Twoey put one foreleg, then the other, into the trailer and finally jumped in. He wondered what he was getting himself into. Before he could think about it too long, the trailer door closed and the van started moving.

Twoey felt the air blow through the van and over his body as he looked out to see the scenery. The trees were moving by so fast that it looked as if he and the van were even speeding past the clouds in the sky. He saw horses feeding and playing in pastures, just beginning to turn green with spring grass. He even saw some cattle look up as the van went by.

On one farm, people were on machines digging up miles and miles of black dirt, making rows and mounds of soil. On another farm, he could see small green plants beginning to grow in the dark rows of dirt that had already been plowed.

"Yeah, this is okay," Twoey said as he looked down to Kidd. He was finally a little excited, thinking forward to his next unknown adventure.

Kidd was too short to see anything, so he lay down and soon the movement of the van rocked him to sleep.

When the van stopped, Amy opened the back doors of the horse trailer and led Twoey out. What he saw next was a world of mass confusion! There were so many things to see all at once! Colts and fillies he had never seen before were walking to his right and left. There were so many people...and so much noise!

Kidd jumped out and took a quick look around at all the activity. He announced to Twoey that he was going exploring and would see him later. He took off running.

Twoey watched him go with a little envy. He wished he could go with his best friend and run around carefree.

Amy let Twoey take a few minutes to adjust to all the new sights and sounds. She then slowly led him in another direction to join the other yearlings.

Twoey had no time to talk or try to make friends with the other horses his age. Each yearling had a human by their side. He watched as one-by-one they were led away from their small gathering place. It wasn't long before it was Twoey's turn.

Amy led him into a big ring that was surrounded by people. Twoey heard an announcer say Amy's name and then his own name! All the people who were watching him clapped.

Twoey felt so proud! He could feel the warmth of pride wash through him—from the bottom of his legs, through his body, into his neck, and to his head, slowly lifting it up.

Amy whispered to him to follow her commands. "This is your first showing, Twoey. The judges will be looking at how well you are trained and how you look, so show off all you want."

With his head held high and his legs strong and sure, Twoey began to do just that. "I'll pretend I'm Diamond Knight," Twoey said to himself. "I'm the biggest, baddest, best champion thoroughbred in all the world...and I'll show everyone how good I am."

Twoey really did feel like king of the thoroughbreds while he was in the ring surrounded by people watching him and applauding. The confidence he felt inside showed on the outside. He followed Amy's commands perfectly, performing with pride apparent in each correct step.

When Twoey was awarded the first-place ribbon, Amy threw her arms around his neck and gave him the biggest hug. Twoey really liked the showing off part of this adventure and was ready to do it again. As Amy began leading him out of the ring, she laughed because she saw in his eyes how much he loved the event, the attention, and the winning! He was still prancing—still showing off.

"I'm afraid that's it for today, Twoey. But you did just great!" Amy was beaming with as much pride as Twoey had in himself. "Remember, you came here just like any other yearling, but you're going home with your first blue ribbon. I am so proud of you! And everyone else noticed you and will remember your name. Twoey. It's a proud name, Twoey."

Twoey could feel his emotions with every beat of his heart—then he felt as if his heart stopped!

Twoey saw her—Angel Eyes. Her mane was braided with

colorful ribbons. She, too, was being led away and she wasn't looking at him. He had to talk to Angel Eyes so he began nudging Amy in her direction.

"What are you doing, Twoey?" Amy asked. "I know you love showing off, but you can't stay here. You've finished competing."

Twoey stopped and refused to move in the direction Amy was trying to lead him. He began pulling Amy in another direction. Then Amy realized what had caught Twoey's attention.

Angel Eyes looked up slowly as Amy led Twoey to her. She lifted her head and nodded as if saying hello. She was so happy to see Twoey that she whinnied. It seemed so long ago that they had been separated. Looking at him, she realized how much she had missed him.

As Amy and Angel Eyes' trainer, Brooke, began talking, Twoey and Angel Eyes moved closer to each other. The lively filly and the young colt looked at each other for a while, noticing how each had grown and matured.

Angel Eyes broke the silence by congratulating him on winning first place.

She had grown but was not as tall as Twoey. He saw that the ribbons in her shiny mane were blowing slightly in the soft breeze. He then noticed a winner's ribbon around her neck. "Looks like you won, too, Angel."

Any awkwardness between the two friends melted away and they became as comfortable with each other as they had been as foals.

"Yes. It was fun being in the show ring, and it was worth all the hard training," Angel told him. "How are you doing with your training? Are you getting ready to begin racing?"

Before Twoey could answer, Amy and Brooke told them it was time to leave. Brooke led Angel away.

Amy watched Twoey as his eyes followed Angel. "We'll stay for a minute and watch her go if you'd like," Amy said. "You'll see her again, Twoey, but you're going to be too busy for visits or play when you get back. You'll start even more intense training and you'll have to concentrate."

Twoey looked at Amy with understanding, but he wanted to keep the vision of Angel Eyes in his mind right now and not think about his future just yet.

When Twoey and Amy approached the horse van, Kidd was sitting by the trailer waiting for them. He ran up to greet them. Kidd was excited to tell Twoey all about his day's adventures and to listen to Twoey's stories. He saw the blue ribbon!

"Twoey, you won, you won!" Kidd kept repeating, over and over again.

Twoey didn't respond, but he slowly ambled up the ramp to the horse trailer and walked in—without fear, without any emotion.

Amy patted his neck and said, "You'll see Angel Eyes again, but she's as busy as you are, training just as hard. You both have goals to achieve." Amy gave her colt a hug and added, "Training won't last forever." She turned and jumped out of the van.

Kidd scooted up into the trailer. He hadn't seen Twoey this quiet since he was separated from his mother. Back then, Kidd had moved into the horse barn and slept at Twoey's stall door to keep his friend company. Kidd had always been able to cheer up Twoey, so he tried again now. "Hey, big-shot winner, what are you all down in the dumps about?"

When Twoey said nothing, Kidd kept going, "Let's see, *what* could it be? I'll recap your day for you, and you can let me know what happened to make you so unhappy. First, your name was announced over a loudspeaker so everyone within a mile could hear it. Then, a big crowd of people cheered. Next, you showed off in the ring. Finally, you won a blue ribbon in your first show. You're right—it has been a depressing day!"

Twoey glared at Kidd. Then he saw the humor in what Kidd had said and relaxed. "It really has been a pretty good day, hasn't it, Kidd?" Twoey told Kidd what Amy had said about his training being stepped up. The more he talked about training to be a racehorse, the more excited he became.

Kidd settled down in a soft corner and was soon asleep.

Twoey was so filled with the emotions of the day that he could not sleep or even rest. He let his mind wander back to the beginning of the day, and he replayed every moment, reliving the events and the emotions. It seemed days ago, instead of mere hours, that he feared stepping into the horse van. He felt again the surge of pride and accomplishment when the crowd had cheered for him and when his name was announced for all to hear. He saw again the happy smile on Amy's face when they were awarded the blue ribbon. In his mind, he pranced out of the arena like a champion again.

Then, seeing Angel Eyes. He had to admit that even with all the cheers and the thrill of winning in the arena, seeing her was the best part of the day. He kept his thoughts on Angel Eyes for the rest of the journey home.

Back in the comfort of his familiar stall, Twoey dreamed that night that he was the center of attention as he proudly pranced around the ring wearing his blue ribbon. The crowd was cheering! In his dream, he saw his mother smiling and nodding her head in approval. Then, all of the images floated from his mind and he could only see Angel Eyes and her mane braided with colorful ribbons. As she walked away, she looked back at him and smiled.

CHAPTER TEN

Run the Race

Amy was right. Twoey was very busy every day now, working with the trainers. The first time they put a saddle on his back, Twoey kicked and lowered his head and tried to throw it off. Soon he realized that it was not coming off, so he began to adjust to the new feeling and the weight. Then they put shoes on him!

After several days, a rider climbed into the saddle on his back. It was a lot of weight, but he remembered seeing Diamond Knight race on the track with the rider on his back. Twoey convinced himself that, if he wanted to be like Diamond Knight, he'd have to accept the rider.

Amy was always nearby, telling Twoey he would be the greatest. He put his fears aside and accepted each new challenge. He didn't want to disappoint Amy. Each day he looked forward to leaving his stall for the training area. He tried to do exactly what the trainers asked him to do.

Besides, Kidd was watching him and Twoey was determined to impress him. While he wanted to do more of the things that he saw the older horses doing, he admitted to Kidd that his legs got tired. He was sweating and breathing hard.

Kidd reassured him that it was all part of his training and conditioning. Twoey knew that Kidd was right. He also listened to the older racehorses tell him to be patient. He had to slowly build up his strength and endurance so that he would be strong enough to run on the oval track. He had to be fast enough to impress the trainers and have the stamina to run the distance.

Finally, Twoey got a day off from training and could go to the pasture. Twoey wanted to forget for just a little while that he was a thoroughbred racehorse in training. He wanted to feel like a foal again. He ran, kicked, rolled in the grass and dirt, and didn't have a care in the world. No thoughts of strength training, no weight to carry around on his back—just play and rest.

Diamond Knight had been watching Twoey go through some of his training. He had a day off, too, and was grazing in the next pasture when he heard the sounds of Twoey playing. He looked up and saw Twoey romping around the field. He couldn't help but watch the young thoroughbred with a bit of envy in his eyes. "Oh to be young, carefree, and have no worries about winning the next competition," Diamond thought to himself.

Twoey could feel someone staring at him and turned to see Diamond Knight. He ran over to the fence to say hello.

"You've grown quite a bit, Twoey," Diamond said, as he observed how much taller and more muscular Twoey had grown. "How are you doing with your training?"

"Oh, it's okay, but I think I can do more. I want to work with the trainers longer, but it seems like we just keep doing the same training over and over again. It's getting boring," Twoey answered honestly.

"Patience has always been a problem for you," Diamond said smiling. "Believe me, the day will come when you will wish that the trainers would not work you so hard. You'll yearn for your younger days, when all you had on your schedule was grazing, playing, and resting."

Twoey noticed that Diamond Knight looked tired. Twoey didn't want to ask him how he was feeling, but instead asked Diamond how his races had been. Had Diamond been anywhere new and exciting?

Diamond responded to the colt with a laugh. "When you get as old as I am and have raced as long as I have, you'll feel that you've been everywhere and seen everything. Instead of looking for something new, you'll be wishing for the familiar sights, smells, and sounds of home."

Twoey looked at Diamond in disbelief. Twoey always imagined Diamond's life as filled with excitement—new adventures every minute.

Diamond noticed Twoey's disappointment, so he said, "You, however, have everything new to look forward to. You'll see many racetracks. The air will be filled with excitement as the announcer shouts your name over the loudspeaker and the crowd cheers." Diamond thought of the little tricks he used to win races and decided to share them with Twoey. "The other horses in the race will look you in the eye and dare you to beat them. But Twoey, you look right back at them and challenge them. There's more to winning a race than just physical speed. A lot of mental play goes into winning as well."

Diamond got a gleam in his eye when he thought of the way he made eye contact with other horses in a race. "When you challenge your opponent with confidence and determination in your eyes, most of them will back down. You'll make them think they don't have a chance to beat you!" Diamond smiled a little as he thought of all his opponents who may have been faster physically but could not compete mentally.

Twoey had stars in his eyes as he visualized the scene.

Diamond noticed Twoey had a faraway look in his eyes. "You're dreaming again, Twoey," Diamond said to snap him back to the present. "Go now and make your dreams come true."

Diamond slowly turned away. The talk with Twoey had made him feel better. Thinking about the racing circuit and explaining it to the young colt cheered the older horse. He realized that he needed a pep talk, too, so that he would get excited again about racing. He was tired. He longed for the energy and enthusiasm of the colt.

* * * *

Twoey celebrated his second birthday with Kidd, Amy, and his equine carrot cake.

Finally, after months of training, the day arrived when Twoey was scheduled to run in his first race. He confided in Kidd how afraid he was. "I've been wanting to race and, now that I can, my legs feel wobbly and my heart is beating too fast. I feel like I can't even walk, let alone run!"

Kidd was nervous, too, but he didn't want Twoey to know it. "Don't think about it," Kidd advised. "Just rely on your training and follow your jockey's movement. It will come naturally, you'll see. When the gate opens, you'll know what to do." Kidd hoped his advice was correct but, in reality, he was just as afraid for Twoey.

As Amy was leading Twoey to the track, he looked back and called for Kidd. "Kidd, you gotta come with me! If you're there, I won't be as afraid. Please?" Twoey pleaded.

Kidd couldn't ignore the panic in Twoey's eyes and so he followed the horse to the gate. Amy laughed when she looked around to see Kidd following them. She had felt Twoey's tension ease as soon as the little goat had stepped in behind them.

"This may be the strangest sight at the track," Amy thought to herself, "but if a little goat can help a thoroughbred become a champion, then it's also the most amazing sight."

As the horses filled all the gates, Twoey still felt the tension but he also felt the excitement. This was the first race for all of them. He gave himself a pep talk, telling himself that he was as well trained as any of them and had just as much chance to win the race. He remembered what his mother had told him: "You are a descendant of the best thoroughbreds in the world—it's in your genes to run." He thought of Diamond Knight who was winning races all over the country. "Diamond thinks I can win," Twoey said, reassuring himself.

"I'll make you proud of me, Mother," Twoey promised as the gate swung open. The bell rang and he sprinted down the track.

Twoey could hardly catch his breath. His heart was pounding. His legs seemed to be going faster than his body. He knew the jockey was on his back, but all he could feel was the wind in his face, the softness of the track as his hooves struck it, and the sensation of flying over the ground. He heard nothing—not the cheering crowd, not the jockey urging him on. He thought about no other horse, just the track ahead of him.

Suddenly, the jockey told him to slow down and take it easy. The race was over.

Just as suddenly, Twoey's senses came flooding back. He heard the cheers from the crowd and the praise from his jockey. He felt the track beneath his hooves as he slowed his pace. Then he saw the other horses in the race. They were behind him.

He had won! He had actually won! He loved the feeling. He was now officially a winning racehorse. Amy would be so proud of him! He couldn't wait to tell Kidd.

Kidd was waiting for him as he left the track. "You did it! You did it!" Kidd kept yelling over and over again.

"You can't believe what it's like to run in a race, Kidd,"

Twoey managed to shout between breaths. "Your mind kind of goes blank and you feel like your body can't keep up with your legs. You're going so fast, the ground seems to disappear. It's unreal!"

Amy ran up to Twoey and gave him the biggest and longest hug he'd ever received. "Twoey, you absolutely FLEW down the track. You were way out front and you won! You won! I'm so happy I think I'm crying." Tears were spilling down Amy's cheeks even as she smiled from ear to ear. "You get cooled down now and I'll see you later. I love you, Twoey!" she called as she turned and ran to her mom and dad.

Kidd walked beside Twoey, listening as Twoey explained every second of the race and how it felt to him. Finally, Twoey said, "You go on to the stall, Kidd, I have a little more work to do. I'll catch up with you there and we'll celebrate."

Reality quickly caught up with Twoey. As he was being rubbed down, his body began to ache a little and his legs felt like all the strength was leaving them. He was suddenly so tired. All he wanted to do was go to the soft bedding in his stall and sleep. He and Kidd would have to celebrate his win tomorrow.

Kidd was already asleep when Twoey got to his stall. Twoey lay down and let his body and legs relax. He, too, was soon fast asleep.

His dreams that night were filled with flying horses. Their legs moved so slowly. He was in front of them, trying to run faster, but his legs wouldn't move as quickly as his mind told them to. But it didn't matter, because he was flying in the air.

CHAPTER ELEVEN

What Happened?

Before long, Twoey finally got his wish and was led through more intense training. His trainer used a high-speed treadmill that forced his legs to run faster to keep up as the track moved beneath him. The best trainers in the world used the treadmill to strengthen their winning thoroughbreds.

Twoey first had to do a half-mile trot, then a one-mile gallop at twenty miles per hour, then a half-mile trot again.

His heart rate was measured and blood samples taken to make sure that his body was responding as it should. He heard his trainer say he had a strong heart, his endurance had increased, and he was ready for a bigger race.

As each day passed, Twoey could feel himself running faster and for longer periods of time. He yearned for the chance to race again.

Finally, race day arrived! Amy came to lead him to the track again. Kidd jumped up with excitement, ready to follow them. But Twoey turned to Kidd and said, "I'm not afraid to go to the gate by myself this time, so you don't need to come with me. I'll see you after I win." He turned away from Kidd to walk beside Amy out of the barn and to the track.

Twoey didn't look back to see the look of disappointment on Kidd's face. He didn't notice when Kidd lowered his head, turned around, and slowly walked away from him to lay in front of his stall.

The sounds, the smells, even the gate felt familiar to Twoey and he was comfortable. But when the gate opened and the bell rang, everything was different! Twoey learned in the first few seconds of the race that it was no fun being behind other horses in a race. He had tried to run around the other horses, but he was penned in on both sides. He got dirt and mud in his mouth, in his eyes, and on his legs. It made him feel heavy, and he couldn't run as fast. He much preferred seeing nothing ahead of him but open track.

When the race was over, there were no cheers for him. He felt tired, dirty, and defeated.

Amy tried to console him after the race, telling him that he wasn't expected to win every race. She tried to encourage Twoey, but he wouldn't pick up his head and the look in his eyes never changed. She promised him that tomorrow he would feel better.

"Man, what happened to you? You look awful!" Kidd was waiting for him when he returned to the barn.

"I can't possibly look as bad as I feel. I was terrible on the track," Twoey admitted. He knew he could talk to Kidd about it. "It seemed everybody ran past me. I could never get in the lead. I don't know what happened but it sure wasn't fun."

Kidd's heart went out to his friend, who was hanging his head, looking defeated. Kidd thought of all the things he could say to try to cheer him up but nothing seemed appropriate right now, so Kidd said, "You must have been pretty bad. You've got dirt all over you."

Twoey's head snapped up in anger. "Well, thanks a lot for your sympathy! There are plenty of horses that laughed at me. I didn't think you would, too."

"You don't need sympathy," Kidd said with kindness. "You need to figure out what went wrong." Kidd tried to make

Twoey realize that he was trying to help him. "Only a good friend can help you be honest with yourself. I'm not going to let you give up, so stop feeling sorry for yourself!" Kidd watched as Twoey relaxed a little and began listening to him. "Something must have been different in the way you raced today," Kidd continued. "Now, let's figure out what it was, so it doesn't happen again."

Kidd was giving Twoey exactly what he needed. His feeling of defeat changed to one of reflection. He began to replay the race in his mind. What had been different?

"I think it's my fault," Kidd joked. "Admit it, Twoey, I'm your good luck charm and I wasn't there. Bet you don't tell me to stay away again."

While Twoey knew that Kidd was joking, he admitted to himself he did want Kidd with him at the track. "Okay, Kidd, so that's one thing that was different. Help me to think of others."

Kidd began walking back and forth, thinking. Then he asked, "Well, how did you feel physically? Were you tired? Did you have sore muscles? Were you out of breath?"

"None of those things." Twoey knew he was in the best condition he'd ever been in.

"Okay, then," Kidd said, with a plan in mind, "let's take it step-by-step through the race."

Twoey replayed the race, second-by-second, for Kidd. "When the gate opened and the bell rang, I sprinted out. But there was already a horse ahead of me, then two, then three. I remember trying to run around them, but I was blocked by horses on either side of me." Twoey felt awful just having to remember it. "The horses in front of me weren't running as fast as I could run, but I couldn't get around them. It was as if they were trying to slow me down so the other horses could pass me."

"They ganged up on you, Twoey," Kidd said, matter of factly.

The realization hit Twoey. "Well, that's not fair," Twoey angrily complained. "If I'm the fastest, then I should win."

"Unfortunately," Kidd explained, "it doesn't always work that way. It's a business, Twoey. If a horse doesn't win at least some races, he'll be sold."

That realization came as a shock to Twoey. He hadn't thought about that. "I wouldn't want any of the horses I compete against to leave this farm." Thinking about not seeing some of his friends again was upsetting. "Even though we try to beat each other, we're still friends." Then Twoey realized that he had lost a race!

"What about me, Kidd? I lost today, will I have to leave?" Twoey couldn't imagine leaving.

Kidd saw the panic in Twoey's eyes. "No, no, Twoey. You've already won a race and I hear you're one of the best two-year-old racehorses on the farm. I think you have a bright future right here!" Kidd then put his head down, as if to butt something, and said, "If they try to take you away from me or this farm, they'll have to fight me!"

Twoey smiled, but he was soon deep in thought again. Twoey remembered something Diamond Knight had said about how hard it is to keep friends when you beat them on the track.

Kidd explained something he had learned on the farm. "Some racehorses join kind of a club," Kidd said. "When I wander around the farm, I hear things. They take care of each other. You're new and you're a threat to them. You may be friends but, when it comes to securing his future, each horse will do what it takes to win."

Twoey was still a little frightened. "But what do I do? I'll have to win, too, or I'll be sent away."

Kidd sat down to think. He looked up at Twoey with a new plan. "Well, then, you'll just have to be first out of the gate before anyone can get in front of you and slow you down. Think, Twoey! What was different *before* the gate opened?"

Twoey closed his eyes to help him remember each moment of the race. "I remember standing at the gate, listening to the crowd. I could smell the mixture of odors from humans, food, and the track. My jockey was talking to me. The bell rang. I saw the gate open and heard the announcer say, 'They're off.'"

"That's it!" Kidd exclaimed with excitement, startling Twoey. "In your first race, you said you didn't hear anything—your mind went blank. This time, you were seeing, smelling, hearing, and thinking too much."

"I wasn't focused on the race, was I?" Twoey admitted to Kidd. "I remember being very comfortable at the gate. I was paying attention to everything that was going on around me. I guess I was distracted."

"You were too comfortable," Kidd said. "You need to be a little excited and a little afraid, but still have confidence that you can win. You're physically strong and prepared. Now, you have to get mentally prepared."

"More workouts!" Twoey grumbled with a smile.

"This one will be easy," Kidd suggested. "I'll be your teacher. Instead of hare-brained ideas, you'll have horse-brained ideas that work." Kidd laughed at his little joke and Twoey laughed with him.

The two friends worked together as a team on Twoey's mental attitude while his trainers worked on his endurance and speed.

CHAPTER TWELVE

Angel's Choice

As Twoey approached the gate for his next race, he tried not to be nervous.

"Concentrate and focus," Kidd kept telling Twoey as they made their way to the starting gate. "Visualize only you in the race and see nothing but track ahead of you. No sounds, no smells, no other sights."

As Twoey entered the gate, he kept saying to himself, "Just follow your legs and fly on the wind. You can fly."

That night, Twoey celebrated his win with Amy, who brought him special treats and kept telling him over and over again how good he was. He also celebrated with Kidd, his mental trainer, by sharing his dinner and treats with him.

Kidd fell asleep in Twoey's stall. Twoey realized that although they may not look alike, they were as close as brothers now.

In Twoey's dreams that night, he and Kidd were smiling, standing side-by-side in the winner's circle as cameras flashed. The flowers around Twoey's neck smelled so good. Kidd was also wearing a circle of flowers around his neck.

* * * *

Twoey had a day off from training and racing, so Amy took both the horse and goat to the pasture. Amy watched her beloved Twoey and his friend Kidd run into the pasture and play as they had done when Twoey was just a foal.

Twoey enjoyed the freedom of playing with no work to do. He had nothing to think about except how warm the sun felt, how green the grass was, and how he missed the carefree days in the pasture.

Twoey hadn't seen his mother in a long time so when he saw her in the mare's pasture, he ran over to the fence to talk to her. She had heard all about his training successes and racing wins and defeat.

"I'm so proud of you, Twoey." His mother just beamed at him, which made Twoey's heart fill with so much love for her. He realized he truly missed his days as a foal beside her. He regretted how anxious he had been to grow up.

"Thanks, Mom. The trainers are keeping me physically fit, and I'm being well fed. Kidd has been helping me stay mentally prepared," he admitted. "I didn't realize that winning races was so much work. But, Mom, it's so much fun!

"Twoey, remember there's more to life than winning every race," Queenie warned. "You've already discovered what it means to have a best friend. You're learning important lessons off the track, too, like caring about others and being kind. Keep doing those things and you'll always be a winner and a champion."

* * * *

Twoey's life became filled with more intense physical training and more racing. Kidd was constantly at his side working on his mental training. Twoey noticed that the more races he won, the harder he trained. He would now gallop four miles every day to build up his stamina. Sometimes his trainers would have him run a two-minute mile, rest for seven minutes, then run a one-minute-fifty-second mile, rest for seven minutes, then run two three-quarter miles with a seven-minute rest in between.

While it was hard work, Twoey confessed to Kidd that he was feeling the difference. He wasn't short of breath as quickly and his heart wasn't pounding as hard. His trainers said his tendons and ligaments were stronger, and his bone density and muscle were developing well.

* * * * *

Twoey hadn't seen Angel Eyes in months. He knew she was in training but she was competing in different races. When he and Kidd were in their stall one night, Twoey asked, "Kidd, you get to run all over the farm. Have you seen Angel Eyes?"

"Yeah," Kidd said in a low voice.

"Well, tell me more, how's she doing? Is she competing in the fillies' races? Does she ask about me?" Twoey impatiently asked.

"She looks just fine," Kidd said before he turned away. He didn't want to tell Twoey anything more about Angel Eyes.

Twoey knew Kidd well enough to know that he was not telling him all that he knew. Twoey decided that, instead of pleading with Kidd to tell him, he would pretend any information about Angel Eyes was not important to him.

"I'm so busy with training, I don't have time to think about anyone else," Twoey lied. "We all have to go our separate ways. She was a good filly and fun to be with, but that's when we were foals. Now that we're grown, I've got bigger and better things to do." Twoey glanced at Kidd. He wanted to see if Kidd was convinced that Twoey had no interest in Angel Eyes.

Twoey knew that Kidd was the farm gossip and couldn't resist telling everything that was going on. But he also knew his friend would try to protect him from learning something that would hurt him.

Kidd took the bait. "Well, I do know a little more about Angel Eyes," Kidd began, walking back toward Twoey. "It seems she really doesn't enjoy the track or all the training like you do. You know, some thoroughbreds just aren't cut out to be a fast racehorse, even if they have the breeding and the heart to run." Kidd was talking a mile a minute. "Look at Snap Dragon. You saw how 'Snappy' was always content to be last. He'd rather look around at what was going on in the stands than concentrate on the track ahead. Now he's with a new owner who's training him to jump fences and be a show horse."

Twoey tried to not let his frustration show when he asked, "So, what's Angel Eyes gonna do?"

"Oh, she's going to a new owner and she'll be trained as a show horse, too. But not in jumping, something else, I think."

"What?!" Twoey exclaimed in disbelief. "She's leaving the farm? How soon? Is she still here? Oh, Kidd, why didn't you tell me?" Twoey cried out.

Kidd then realized how Twoey had tricked him into thinking he no longer cared about Angel Eyes. The damage was done. Twoey now knew that Angel Eyes was leaving.

"Things are changing so fast, Kidd," Twoey said with sadness in his voice. "I wonder if I'll ever see Angel Eyes again?"

Kidd heard him and asked in a timid voice, "Do you want to see her?"

Twoey's head snapped up. "Can I? Can you take me to her?"

With pride in his voice, Kidd said, "I can do anything. C'mon." He opened the stall door and led Twoey out of the barn.

Twoey and Kidd quietly sneaked into the fillies' barn. While Kidd stood watch outside, Twoey found Angel's stall. He saw her standing in the back corner of her stall, turned away from the door.

Twoey whispered, "Hi ya, Angel."

Angel's head whipped around toward the door in surprise. "Twoey, what are you doing here? How did you get in? You'll get in trouble if they find you here."

"Kidd and I were bored and thought we'd take a walk around the farm. We do that a lot," Twoey lied. "I've been so busy with training and all I haven't had time to visit you so we thought we'd make a midnight run over here."

Angel Eyes could see right through the lie Twoey was telling, but she was so glad to see him, she didn't care.

"Oh, Twoey. I'm so glad you came," Angel said. "I've wanted to tell you how proud I am of you. You're the talk of the farm. You are becoming a real champion racehorse."

She was so easy to talk to, Twoey thought. He told her, "Well, after losing a race, I decided I never wanted to do that again, so I've been training really hard."

They talked for a while about what some of their other friends were doing. Finally, Angel said, "Twoey, what's on your mind? You didn't come here to chat."

Twoey looked into her soft brown eyes. He had to know. "Kidd said you are leaving?"

Angel looked down. This was going to be hard to explain. "Racing is not for me, Twoey. I don't enjoy the intense training like you do, and I'm not a competitor. This is a racing farm. Those who don't race don't belong here. That's a fact and I accept it." She looked up. "You must accept it, too."

"But where will you go? What will you do?" Twoey asked in alarm.

Angel had a twinkle of excitement in her eyes as she

explained. "Last week, a mother and little girl came to meet me. They are very nice and liked me a lot. They told me they have a wonderful farm with green pastures. I won't have to train to race anymore. The little girl wants me to be her show horse. They are going to train me in an event called *dressage*. I'll have my mane braided with ribbons and I'll be groomed so my coat glistens. I'll be treated like a queen, Twoey." She looked at him, trying to get him to understand. "It's what I want."

Twoey saw the happiness and hope in her eyes. "You'll be great no matter what you decide to do," he finally said, meaning it. "There are champions in lots of sports, not just racing," Twoey said, trying to support her decision to leave.

"Thanks for understanding, Twoey."

"How soon will you go?" Twoey asked, unable to hide his sadness.

"They're picking me up this weekend. Since I won't be racing anymore, I don't have to go to training. I'll be in the pasture located next to the mare's pasture, so it will give me a chance to spend some time with my mom and Queenie. They're very excited about my new career."

Twoey wished he could share her excitement. All he felt was an ache in his heart. His Angel was leaving. He was determined not to let her see the sorrow he was feeling.

"I'm excited for you, too, Angel. It will be fun to be in training for something new. And to think, you'll be in the show ring!"

"Thanks for coming tonight, Twoey. I was hoping I'd get the chance to see you again. You're very special to me. I won't miss the farm, but I will miss you."

Angel put her head further out the stall door and nuzzled Twoey's neck. Then she turned away. She didn't want to make the good-bye more difficult than it was.

Twoey walked slowly and quietly out of the barn to where Kidd was waiting. They walked in silence back to their stall. Twoey was so grateful to have his loyal friend by his side. With everything else changing in his life, he depended on the one thing that was constant—and that was Kidd.

CHAPTER THIRTEEN

The Knight Falls

Twoey was on a winning streak and he was only two years old. When he won the Breeders' Cup for Juveniles in early November, he earned the title of champion.

Diamond Knight continued to help Twoey with racing. They talked whenever they were in adjoining pastures. Twoey was learning a lot from him about racing strategy— things like body language. He learned that by holding his head up and arching his neck he could send the message that he intended to win. Diamond said body language might break some of the other horses' confidence and give Twoey an extra edge.

Twoey and Diamond Knight were scheduled to race on the same day but in different cities. Diamond Knight was entered in a big race called the Cigar Mile Handicap at Aqueduct Race Course in New York. The winner earned $350,000.

Twoey was competing in a $200,000 Kentucky Jockey Club race for two-year-olds at Churchill Downs in Kentucky. Twoey knew he had to concentrate and focus on his own race, but his mind kept wandering to Diamond Knight's big race. He knew how badly Diamond wanted to win this one! Twoey was so thankful for Kidd's constant companionship and mentoring that he often wished Diamond had someone close to him to help him through the rough times.

When the bell rang and the racetrack gates opened at Churchill Downs, Twoey focused on his own competition. He had to do his best for one-and-a-sixteenth mile. His racing technique was becoming predictable. He'd get out in front, stay on the rail, and cross the finish line first. Then he would enter the winner's circle for pictures and praise. But Twoey never took it for granted, remembering with dismay how he was covered with mud and dirt after he lost a race.

However, after today's win Twoey felt anxious, although he didn't know why. As he walked to cool down and meet up with Amy and Kidd, he heard the track announcer say that a horse had been critically injured in the Cigar Mile Handicap Stakes Race at Aqueduct. Twoey's legs felt like crumbling. His heart began pounding very fast and he was sweating. It was not from the race, but from the sudden panic he was feeling. One look at Amy and his fears were confirmed. He knew then that the injured horse was Diamond Knight. Amy had heard about the tragedy while Twoey was winning his race. Kidd had heard, too. The three of them walked in silence, side-by-side, back to the barn.

Amy tried to reassure Twoey. She stroked his neck. "Maybe the injury isn't as bad as we first heard. Diamond's in good health and will heal quickly, and there is so much new medical technology that can help him." Amy tried with all her heart to believe what she was saying.

Twoey heard the words but couldn't accept the hope Amy was trying to give to him. He didn't want to eat. He just wanted to lie down in a corner and pretend that today never happened. The champion was down.

Kidd knew that there was nothing he could say to ease Twoey's sorrow. He just stayed next to Twoey so that he would not be alone.

Twoey closed his eyes, trying to forget the traumatic event of the day. He finally fell asleep. That night Twoey dreamed of Diamond Knight. He saw the black stallion come up behind him and nudge him along. When Twoey tried to stop, Diamond kept nudging him, telling him it was time for him to go on by himself. As Diamond stood watching, Twoey walked away. When Twoey turned around to say good-bye, Diamond was gone.

* * * *

The next day, Amy came by Twoey's stall with some carrots, his favorite treat. "I thought maybe this would cheer you up a little." But Twoey wouldn't even sniff them. She felt so sorry for the horse. She could tell he was upset by Diamond Knight's injury. Even Kidd looked unhappy. She knew Kidd could usually get Twoey's spirits up—but not today.

"How would you like to go out to the pasture, Twoey?" Amy asked. "Your mother's in the next field. She's sad over Diamond's injury. Maybe you can cheer each other up a little." As Amy opened the stall door, she said, "You, too, Kidd, c'mon."

Twoey thought that if he could just talk to his mother about Diamond, he would feel better. As soon as he was in the pasture, Twoey ran over to the fence to see her.

Queenie could see the sorrow in his eyes and explained to him, "Injury is a grim part of the racing world, Twoey. Regardless of how physically and mentally prepared you are, unpredictable things can happen to end your career."

It was something Twoey had never realized before and it frightened him. He had thought the horses that got injured brought it on themselves by not training properly or refusing to eat the right foods.

"Have you heard how badly he's injured?" Twoey asked.

"Yes, it's bad. He'll never race again. But Twoey, he will live and be able to walk after surgery."

Twoey was relieved to know that Diamond Knight was alive, even if he couldn't race.

"There's more, Twoey," his mother said reluctantly, not wanting to hurt him further but knowing he needed the truth. "They're taking him to Rood & Riddle Equine Hospital in Lexington, Kentucky. It's one of the best in North America," she continued, as Twoey watched her closely, hanging on every word. "He'll get the rehabilitation he requires to heal his physical injuries. But he needs other healing. Emotional healing. He's depressed and doesn't have the will to get better." Queenie sighed but continued, "They're sending me to be with him. They think I can help him recover." Queenie had dreaded telling Twoey this, but she continued, "I'll be leaving tomorrow."

"No, Mother, no," Twoey cried with alarm. "You can't go. What will I do without you here on the farm? Tell them to take me, too. I can help Diamond and help you. I'll be good. You'll be proud of me," Twoey pleaded, hopeful she would say yes.

"I'll always be proud of you, Twoey, as will Diamond. We'll both follow your racing career with pride." Queenie tried to give Twoey some reassurance. "Remember when we were separated when you were just six months old and I told you that I would always be in your heart? Well, you've got a big heart, Twoey, and Diamond can live in your heart, too. We'll always be with you."

Later, in the darkness of his stall, Twoey felt like his heart was breaking. But when he opened his heart to put Diamond Knight there with his mom and Angel Eyes, he suddenly felt stronger and filled with love.

CHAPTER FOURTEEN

A Plot Against Kidd

Twoey relied on Kidd more than ever, and Kidd valued their strong friendship. He confessed to Kidd, "You're not only my best friend and supporter, but you've become as close as family, like a brother." It made no difference to Twoey that Kidd was not a thoroughbred and that they looked nothing alike. He ignored the laughter and teasing from the other thoroughbreds. He decided they were jealous because they didn't have a best friend. Kidd would stand by him when it seemed his whole world was crumbling.

Twoey's third birthday brought the traditional carrot cake by Amy, which he promptly shared with Kidd. Amy talked to him. She laughed as she remembered the first time she saw him just after he was born and he knocked her over!

Twoey thought back to his days as a young foal, when he was still with his mom, Angel Eyes, and Diamond Knight. He didn't want to think of the past with sadness, so he remembered how much fun they had together. He needed to think of the future and of the races ahead of him.

Less than a week after his birthday, Twoey was entered in the Appleton Handicap, an important one-mile race for three-year-old thoroughbreds at Gulfstream Park in Florida.

The trainers were nervous. It was going to be a long, tiring ride in the horse van. A lot of money was at stake with the winner of the race winning $150,000. The money would help support the horse farm. Twoey's trainers put their reputation on the line, based on whether or not Twoey won. They didn't want anything to interfere with Twoey's concentration. They felt Kidd distracted the horse and they wanted his full attention on what he had to do. Even more than that, they thought the goat was an embarrassment to them. So, after taking Twoey out of his stall, the trainers locked Kidd in the stall.

"He'll be back in a couple of days, Kidd," the trainers said. "You just stay here and behave yourself." Then they led Twoey to the horse van while Kidd let out several ear-splitting cries. But the trainers had not counted on Twoey's reaction. Twoey would not go quietly. He kicked and reared and whinnied for Kidd.

"What's going on?" Amy asked the trainers as she ran to find out why Twoey was upset. "What's wrong with Twoey?"

"He apparently wants that silly goat to go with him in the van. It's going to be a long ride, and a goat just doesn't belong at a big race like this," the trainer tried to explain. Then the trainer said what was really on his mind. "Look, it may have been cute to have a goat with Twoey when he was young, but it's time he grew up and acted like a champion."

Amy had trouble holding her temper as she snapped back, "Don't you ever even THINK that Twoey is not acting like a champion. He's proved it, time and time again." It was apparent to Amy that Twoey was in a panic without Kidd, and he would be unsuccessful at the Florida race without his constant companion.

As the trainers tried to calm Twoey, Amy went into the barn and opened the stall door. Kidd quickly bolted out of the stall and out of the barn, running past Twoey and jumping into the van. No way was he being left behind.

Seeing Kidd in the van, Twoey calmly stepped inside.

"You can't do this, Miss Amy," the trainers complained. "We'll be laughed at when we pull up."

"Well," Amy answered, "you can tell anyone at the track that this is a new training procedure for the J.R. Brand Ranch. Kidd goes wherever Twoey goes. That's the rule. And after Twoey wins, no one will be laughing."

* * * *

On race day, with Kidd watching from the starting gate, Twoey was like a flash of lightning when the gate sprang open. He took the lead and kept it.

The win was a critical one for the J.R. Brand Ranch. It not only gave them the money they needed to continue and improve the racing farm, but it gave them the prestige of having a champion in a top Florida race. The win was also important psychologically. After Diamond Knight's career-ending injury that left everyone depressed, it was good to smile, laugh, and consider a bright racing future for Twoey.

The win also meant that the traveling arrangements were settled—once and for all. Twoey and Kidd always traveled together. There was never again a question. They were a team, no matter how important the race.

While the thoroughbred and the goat were content, some of the trainers were still not happy with the arrangement. They felt that Twoey should be more disciplined—forced to perform and win races without depending on a goat. And the trainers didn't like taking orders from Amy, a teenage owner. They started plotting a way out—a way to get rid of Twoey and the goat.

The trainers would find a buyer for Twoey and send the horse and the goat away from the J.R. Brand Ranch. It wouldn't be hard. Twoey's success on the track had attracted the attention of many buyers.

CHAPTER FIFTEEN

Amy's Dilemma

"**B**ut, Daddy, you can't sell Twoey!" Amy cried. "He's bringing in lots of money for the ranch and, if he can make money for someone else, he can make money for us. I know you've always told me that horse racing is a business and I shouldn't get attached to the horses, but Twoey's special!" Tears filled Amy's eyes. "It's a miracle he even lived. I helped nurse him to health. I just can't let him go. Please, please, don't sell him," Amy pleaded. She hugged her dad for comfort and let the tears fall.

"Amy, you know that I would never hurt you, and I try to make you happy. But think about it, you'll soon be heading off to college. You've grown and you're getting ready for further education. Like you, it's time for Twoey to move on to better training and greater racing opportunities than we can give him here," her father explained.

Seeing that Amy was beginning to understand, he continued, "Twoey is ready to graduate—to compete in bigger races all over the country. We can't change our entire racing program here at the ranch to concentrate on one horse, even though I know he is very special. You can take pride in knowing you've helped make him a high-priced champion. With the money we're getting for him, we can buy five other horses that we can train to become winners."

Amy knew any more arguments about keeping Twoey were useless. He would be sold for a lot of money and he would leave the ranch for a bigger racing stable. However, she did think of one more argument that would help Twoey.

"Promise me one thing, Daddy?" Amy pleaded through her tears.

"I'll try my best, Amy. What is it?"

"Promise me that Kidd will go with Twoey. That the new owners will take care of him, too, and never separate Twoey and Kidd?"

Amy's dad had to laugh. "I don't think anything or anyone could separate those two. It won't take the new buyer long to figure out that Twoey won't run, or won't do anything for that matter, without Kidd. If they want to keep a champion racehorse, they'll have to keep the goat! But, yes, Amy, that's a promise I can keep." He kissed her forehead to seal the promise.

* * * *

Twoey turned his head outside the stall door. He looked to the left and then to the right. "Do you see Amy yet, Kidd?"

Kidd was outside the stall, also looking to the left and right. Amy was about an hour late with their daily treats. "No. But I know she'll come. She never misses giving us our treats." Then Kidd spotted her entering the barn. "See, here she comes now."

Twoey did his happy prance as he always did to greet Amy. He lifted his head up and down as if to say, "Howdy, Amy, how ya doin'?" Kidd stood by patiently, his mouth watering in anticipation of the sweet treat.

Twoey sensed a difference in Amy immediately. She was not the happy, skipping girl he always saw. There had been tears in her eyes, and the sadness was still there. When Amy opened the stall door, Twoey nuzzled her. She put her hands on Twoey's neck as a way of hugging him.

Amy wanted to stay that way forever. She wanted time to stand still, or even turn back to a time when Twoey was a foal, when she would watch him romp in the meadow with Kidd and his mother. If she had known what the future held, if she had thought there was a possibility Twoey would be sold and leave the ranch, would she have worked so hard to help him become the champion thoroughbred racehorse he was today? She stepped back to look into Twoey's big brown eyes.

"Oh, Twoey, did I do the right thing?" she asked as her eyes swelled with tears. "I wanted you to be the best. I wanted you to prove to those people who thought you wouldn't make it that you could become great." The tears started falling over her cheeks. "And you did. You have become the best." She felt torn inside. She was so proud of Twoey and his successes. Yet, because he became a champion, he now would be taken away from her.

She looked at him carefully and, for the first time, saw him differently. Amy focused on Twoey's strong neck and his head with the small white star. She saw his majestic, muscular build and his glistening dark bay-colored coat that looked black. He had well-trimmed hooves and well-trained legs. At 16.3 hands, he towered over her. Amy suddenly saw him as a champion, not the growing colt she had known.

She admitted to herself as she said to Twoey, "You are a champion thoroughbred, Twoey. You have achieved what we only dreamed of when you were born." Amy reached up and touched Twoey's head and neck. Her tears continued as she accepted the fact that she would have to let Twoey go. She would try to make him understand.

"You've outgrown us, Twoey," she quietly said to her beloved horse. "It's time for you to prove yourself in bigger competitions and have the opportunity to win the biggest races in this country and all over the world."

Twoey listened to what she was saying. He wished he could tell her he didn't want to see the world. He only wanted to see her and the familiar sights of the ranch where he'd been born, where he'd grown, trained, and had friends. All he could do was shake his head. Maybe she would see he was saying, "No, no, no. Don't send me away."

As she patted his head, she said, "You won't be alone. Father says Kidd can go with you to your new home." Twoey lowered his head and Amy put her cheek against him. "I'll never forget you, Twoey," she promised. "And I'll follow all your races. When I get a break from school, I'll try to come to see you and Kidd wherever you are. I know someday we'll be together again."

She moved away from him a little to look into his eyes and smiled. "Maybe when I get my degree and I'm a veterinarian, I can bring you back home or get a job at the ranch where you'll be staying." She had to give herself something to hope for, something to hold onto. She gave Twoey his treats for the last time. She would not say good-bye.

Twoey could not eat. As Kidd munched on the treats, Amy turned, walked out of the stall, and closed the door. Their eyes met again. They both understood. Understood the love they felt for each other, understood that their lives were about to change, understood why the decision had to be made, and, most of all, understood that they had such a strong bond that they would never really be apart. One day, they might be able to see each other again.

Kidd had not been listening. He was too interested in eating his treats. When he glanced up at Twoey, the thoroughbred had a faraway look in his eyes. "Well, what was that all about?" Kidd asked, as if it were a joke.

104

When Twoey didn't answer or even look at him, Kidd got annoyed. "Hey, Buster! Snap out of it! What's with you, anyway? You haven't even touched your treats."

Twoey stood facing the far corner of his stall. He wished he could cry. He was leaving his home, leaving the other horses he had come to know, leaving the humans who cared for him and loved him. Leaving Amy.

He was afraid. Would he be loved at his new home, or just be a horse who ran fast? Twoey knew his speed came from his legs and his strength. But his speed also came from his heart. How could he run fast when his heart wasn't in it?

Kidd quietly came over to his friend and stood beside him. "Something's wrong, isn't it, Twoey?" Kidd asked, with quiet dread in his voice. "You might as well tell me now and get it over with, so I can be sad with you."

"I have to leave here, Kidd. I've been sold to a new owner. Amy says it's a bigger ranch. It has the most advanced training facilities to help improve my speed and endurance even more, so I can enter the biggest races in the world."

Kidd could only stare at Twoey, not believing what he was hearing.

"I've always wanted to be the best thoroughbred racer in the world, but I always thought I would stay here," Twoey said, unable to hide his grief. Twoey wondered aloud, "If I hadn't won every race, would I have been able to stay? If I hadn't trained as hard to be the best, would I have to leave?"

"You couldn't be anything but a champion, Twoey," Kidd told him. "You never would have backed off your training or slowed down in a race. It's in your blood and your heart to be a winner."

"Yeah, and look where it got me," Twoey answered sadly.

Kidd stood as tall as he could and, with Twoey's head hanging down in sadness, Kidd was able to look him in the eye. "Well, look at it like a brand new adventure," Kidd said with hope. "Let's face it, Twoey, we've explored every inch of this ranch. There's hardly anything new here to see anymore. We'll have a whole new ranch to turn upside down," Kidd said enthusiastically.

Twoey told him, "Amy said that you can come with me. But Kidd, when they come to take me away, you can hide. You don't have to go. I'm sure they won't make you leave. I don't know what's ahead for me. It's a gamble you don't have to take if you don't want to."

Kidd laughed. "What? Break up the team just when we're ready to see the world and win some really BIG money? I wouldn't miss it!" And Kidd meant every word of it.

Twoey had to smile at his little friend. "What would I do without my constant sidekick?"

"You'd probably still be eating dirt, bringing up the rear on the racetrack," Kidd teased.

Twoey started to feel better. "Wait until the new place gets a load of us!" Twoey laughed. "They don't know what they're getting into! Now, let's get some sleep. We have a long journey ahead of us."

Twoey closed his eyes, but sleep would not come. He feared the journey would be difficult. He hadn't been this afraid since his first night without his mother. Amy had tried to reassure him that this new life would be a good one. She had reminded him that Diamond Knight had left the ranch to compete in bigger races. He succeeded and returned.

He thought of his mom and the daily horse lessons when he was a foal. They were all important in his life. What they had given him helped him become a champion, not only physically, but a champion in his heart. She was gone from his life, but forever living in his heart.

Twoey looked down at Kidd and heard the soft sounds

of Kidd's sleep. They were peaceful sounds. Twoey suddenly felt calm inside. He wasn't alone in this new adventure. He was bringing a whole team with him—his mom, Diamond Knight, Angel Eyes, Amy—and, of course, Kidd.

PART TWO

Twoey and Kidd's New Life

CHAPTER SIXTEEN

The Journey Begins

The horse trailer arrived at dawn the next morning to pick up Twoey and Kidd. Amy saw it arrive from her bedroom window. She had been dressed for hours, not wanting to miss seeing Twoey before he left and yet dreading it with all her heart—the hour, the minute, and the second he would be taken away from the ranch.

She was torn between the choice to see him or to stay in her room. She knew she would cry and she didn't want Twoey to remember his last look at her and the farm to be one of sadness. Even as her tears began falling again, she knew she had to see him. Somehow she had to convince him, and herself, that this was the opportunity of a lifetime and the beginning of happy new adventures.

Amy heard the gentle tap on her door. "Amy, are you awake?" her dad whispered. Should she answer and face the next question, or pretend she was asleep and avoid going to the barn with her dad? She made the decision—the only one that was right for her and for Twoey.

"Yes, I'm awake. I'm coming, Dad."

As father and daughter walked to the barn and Twoey's stall, they did not talk. Each of them had their own special love and admiration for Twoey. Each wanted to keep their personal thoughts and memories inside themselves of these last few moments that Twoey spent at the ranch. They would talk—and share—later.

Twoey heard Amy and her dad walking down the aisle of the barn, walking toward his stall. He did not go to the stall door to look out and greet them as he usually did. He did not want them to come for him this time. He looked down at Kidd. That sight at least made him smile because Kidd, in his predictable way, was curled up, sound asleep, oblivious to the drastic change that would be taking place in their lives in just a few seconds.

Kidd, though, was not really asleep. He had kept his eyes closed and tried to remain calm throughout the night as he listened to Twoey pace back and forth across their stall. He had hoped that, if Twoey thought he was asleep and not worried about their future, Twoey would relax. Kidd knew that Twoey didn't want to talk about leaving the ranch—leaving Amy and his trainers, his friends, and the comfort of his daily routine. Neither of them knew where they were going or what to expect. They could only worry about it, and talking about it would make them worry even more. They had to trust Amy and her dad and believe them when they said that Twoey and Kidd were going to a better ranch.

However, in his heart, Kidd didn't believe them. "What could be better than this?" he had thought to himself. Kidd realized that Twoey had stopped walking and was standing still in the back of his stall, hardly breathing. Kidd heard the footsteps walking toward the stall. If he kept his eyes closed, perhaps they would go away. Then he heard the stall door open.

Amy swallowed her emotions and put a smile on her face as she looked at Twoey. "Hi there, big guy." She walked over and put her arms around his neck.

Kidd jumped up and joined them. Amy kept one hand on

Twoey's neck and patted Kidd's head with her other hand. "Hi, little man."

Amy's dad stood at the stall door, letting the loving scene of his daughter, the champion thoroughbred, and the goat soak into him. He wanted to remember it forever.

Twoey nuzzled Amy's neck and nipped at the back of her jacket as he had done so many times before. Amy laughed. Twoey looked in her eyes. He recognized the emotions he saw in them. They mirrored the emotions he was feeling. They shared a special language between them, and they both understood what each other was saying and feeling today.

Amy smiled at him again. "C'mon, Twoey, it's time to begin your new life."

As she turned, Twoey walked behind her, following her out of his stall. It had begun. He was walking away from the stall where he spent his first night away from his mother, where he had returned after a full day of training, where he had rested after speeding on the racetrack, and where he had celebrated his wins with Kidd and Amy. He was walking away from the only life he had known. He wanted to turn back, but he kept walking.

Kidd followed them. As he looked ahead, he tried to think of it as a parade. Leading the parade was Mr. Brand, then Amy, then Twoey, and himself. Kidd lifted his head, and, imitating the fancy walk he had seen some horses do, he lifted his legs as if marching. Kidd suddenly realized he had confidence in the future and, feeling that confidence, he began to look forward to the new adventure he and Twoey would soon begin.

The foursome walked out of the barn and toward the driver of the horse trailer who would take Twoey and Kidd to their new home.

The driver looked at Twoey. "Wow, he's a beauty!" He

walked around Twoey, who stood very still and straight as if on display. "Wait till Maxwell sees him!" the driver commented. "We knew his papers and track record were excellent, but he sure has the looks to back up his paperwork."

The driver then turned to Amy and her dad. They were standing very straight and still. He recognized the look of anxiety he had seen before on the faces of owners who gave up a thoroughbred they had raised from birth.

"Don't you worry, now. I'll take good care of him. He will be treated like a king. Mr. Maxwell thinks of his racehorses as royalty, so this guy will get the best of everything." The driver tried to reassure them. "You can come visit him at any time," he promised.

Amy gave Twoey another big hug and a smile as she said, "I will come visit you, Twoey. We'll see each other again. And I know we'll be together again every day, just like we have been, someday." Someday, Amy thought to herself. She would hold onto that thought, that hope, that promise. Someday.

Kidd had been totally ignored by the driver. He quietly walked by the group and jumped into the horse trailer. As the driver walked toward the trailer with Amy, her dad, and Twoey, the driver saw Kidd. He turned to Mr. Brand.

"My papers don't say anything about hauling a goat!" he protested.

Amy fearfully looked at her father.

Mr. Brand was calm as he said, "The sales agreement insists that the goat goes wherever the horse goes. So, if you refuse to take the goat, the sales agreement is voided and you don't get the horse."

The driver looked at Mr. Brand, uncertain about what to do.

Mr. Brand continued, "If you'd like, I'll call your boss to

make sure he knows why he's not getting his million-dollar horse."

The indecision left the driver's face.

"We're in agreement, now?" Mr. Brand concluded.

"All right, then. Load 'em up! Horse AND goat!" the driver grumbled.

Twoey got in next to Kidd. Amy and her father watched as the trailer door was shut and the van pulled away.

Watching Twoey leave helped Amy make an important decision about her own life. She was now sixteen and needed to prepare for the next chapter in her life, just as Twoey was preparing for a new chapter in his life. In the quiet of her bedroom, Amy started writing down her own goals for her future and the steps she needed to take to reach them.

She loved thoroughbreds. She loved the excitement, even the disappointments she experienced being a part of a thoroughbred ranch. Spending time with the horses—helping in the foaling, and the training, and the medical treatment—was a part of her life. No, not just a part of her life, she admitted, it was the best part of her life. She wanted it to be her future, too.

Included in her goals for the future was getting Twoey back. To get Twoey back, she had a lot of preparation and training to do herself. Just like Twoey, she thought, with a smile. "So, Twoey," she said aloud in a promise, "while you are away from me, training and competing in the top races in the country, I'll be training to become the best thoroughbred ranch owner and equine veterinarian in the country. We both have a lot of work to do, but when we've both accomplished our goals, we'll be together again."

Amy was suddenly happy again. She felt in control of her and Twoey's futures. She jumped up from her study desk and ran downstairs to find her dad. He was sitting at the breakfast table drinking coffee. When he looked up to see her smiling, his guilt over selling Twoey eased somewhat.

"Dad, I need your help," Amy began. "I want you to start teaching me everything about running a thoroughbred ranch...and I want to start today."

CHAPTER SEVENTEEN

Colt of the Year

Twoey and Kidd tried to get as comfortable as possible, but it was a long ride and they both bounced around as the trailer went over rough roads. They didn't talk much, both afraid that, if they said anything at all, their fear would show.

They finally arrived at their new home. As Twoey was being led out of the trailer, he heard someone yell, "Why did you bring that goat? Couldn't you have dropped him off somewhere?"

"Look," the driver yelled back, "I did what I was told. That horse doesn't go anywhere without that goat. And my advice to you is, you'd better keep them together or the boss will have you dropped off somewhere."

Kidd stood underneath Twoey's belly, his little legs shaking with fear.

"Stay right with me, Kidd," Twoey reassured him, even though he was afraid, too. Twoey was ready to kick or bite anyone who came after Kidd. His ears back, ready to defend, Twoey had a look of defiance in his eyes.

Two men approached them, carefully looking over Twoey.

"Looks like he made the trip okay, Mr. Maxwell. I'll put him up in stall 3 and get him settled with a nice dinner," the trainer said.

"By the looks of it, you'd better make that dinner for two, Louie," Lucas Maxwell laughed. He looked at the sales agreement. "This says the goat's name is Kidd. They warned me that the horse and goat were inseparable." He saw Kidd trying to hide behind Twoey's legs. "But it looks like the goat is attached to the horse's belly. What a pair!" He was still laughing as he walked away. "Can't wait to see what happens on the training track tomorrow."

Louie was laughing, too, as he led Twoey and Kidd to stall 3. "Hey, Kidd, maybe we can train you to be a jockey and you can ride on top instead of walking underneath." He laughed even more at the image that brought to mind.

* * * *

As Twoey and Kidd settled down for the first night in their new home, they tried to encourage each other.

"Our new owner, Mr. Maxwell, seems nice," Twoey said to Kidd.

"And Louie seems okay," Kidd replied.

"Wonder how many horses they have here? I wonder what training equipment they'll put me on? Do you suppose they have a big green pasture for us to run in?" Twoey thought of a million questions. Most would be answered when the sun came up.

"It's been a long day. I'm going to sleep and you should, too," Kidd said. "They're not going to let you lie around in a pasture and get fat. They'll start training you their way tomorrow." With that, Kidd closed his eyes and fell asleep.

Twoey envied the way Kidd could sleep through any crisis.

"Tomorrow," Twoey said to himself as he looked around his new stall. "Yesterday," Twoey thought. They were simple words with so much emotion in each one. "Yesterday, I was happy and loved, with Mom, Diamond, Angel, and Amy. I'll have to keep yesterday in my memory and in my heart."

Thinking of those who loved him made him feel better and he didn't feel so alone. He would get some sleep now. Tomorrow and all of its unknowns would come soon enough.

*　*　*　*

At the first hint of daylight, the barn came alive with the sounds of trainers and handlers opening stall doors and horses being led out.

It seemed to Twoey that only five minutes had passed since he closed his eyes. Had he slept at all last night?

"What's all the racket?" Kidd grumbled as he tried to open his sleepy eyes. "It's not even daylight! Tell them to go back to sleep, Twoey. I'm going to close my eyes for just a few minutes more."

"Well, Kidd," Twoey said with enthusiasm. "Tomorrow is now today. I have yesterday safely tucked away in my memory, so I guess I'm ready to begin today's new adventure." Twoey looked at his little buddy who was trying to curl up again for a little more sleep. "If you don't want to miss it, I suggest you shake the sleep away and get up."

"Who gave you a new attitude, Mister Sunshine?" Kidd teased. "Last night you were all gloom and doom."

"Well, I decided to take the advice of a very intelligent being who told me that 'attitude' is everything. Do you remember saying that, Kidd?"

"Yeah, I do. Now, why don't you give me an attitude lesson." Twoey and Kidd's laughter could be heard all over the barn.

"Well, aren't you the bright-eyed guy this morning?" Louie said as he opened Twoey's stall gate. "I have a feeling we're going to be good friends, especially if you keep up that happy attitude. I sure hate having to work with horses that have a mean streak."

As Louie led Twoey out of his stall, he looked at Kidd. "Well, aren't you coming to check out the ranch and see Twoey's training? You'll soon get to know your way around, even though it is a pretty big ranch."

As they walked out of the barn, Louie talked to Twoey as if he were a human, asking him how he slept, if he liked his bedding in the stall, if he enjoyed his dinner. Twoey nodded his head a couple of times, just so Louie would know he was paying attention. He liked Louie's voice.

Twoey went through some light exercises to get back in shape after his long ride. Then he heard Louie tell his rider to "breeze" him. Twoey loved this exercise on the training track. He was allowed to run as fast as he wanted to run. Twoey loved feeling the breeze in his face and the freedom to run, full out, at his own pace.

When he had finished, Louie praised him. "Wanted to show off on your first day, did you? Well, Twoey, you did it. If you can keep racing at that speed, nobody can catch you." He stroked the thoroughbred's neck and Twoey felt comfort at his touch.

That night in their stall, Twoey admitted to Kidd, "I'm not afraid of being here anymore, and I've decided to put my trust in Louie. I think he really cares about me."

"I can't argue with that. He even cares about me," Kidd responded. "He gave me special treats and never scolded me when I got into mischief. He actually thinks I'm funny. He said I make him laugh."

Twoey slept soundly that night. He dreamed of the J.R. Brand Ranch, Amy, his mom, Diamond Knight, and Angel Eyes. They were all together again. Then, one by one each began walking away into a misty fog. Out of the fog, Louie was coming toward him. Twoey started walking to meet him.

* * * *

Twoey's new owner wasted no time in entering the three-year-old colt in some of the highest paying races in the country. With Louie training him, Twoey soon earned the reputation of being unbeatable on the track.

Twoey responded to each new level of intense training. He was running longer distances and training for longer periods of time. He could tell that all the hard work was worth it when he got to each race. The races were becoming more intense as well. He was competing against the fastest thoroughbreds in the world now, but he loved the tension, the excitement, and the challenge.

When Twoey finished his racing season as a three-year-old, he was awarded Colt of the Year! Ribbons and flowers were put around his neck at a special ceremony, but the best award was Amy. She had come to see him get the honor. When Amy put her arms around his neck, it was a better feeling than all the ribbons, flowers, awards, and winner circles.

Twoey knew for a fact then that Amy would really always be with him and never forget him. Even though she wasn't *with* him, she was still thinking of him and was proud of him. In that moment, he decided he would work even harder to make her even more proud of him.

CHAPTER EIGHTEEN

Up, Up, and Away

On the morning of Twoey's fourth birthday, he and Kidd were still sleeping in their stall when Louie opened the door. "Hey, sleepyhead, it's time to get up—even if you do have a day off today from training."

Twoey walked over to Louie, while Kidd stayed curled up on the floor. But Kidd did manage to open one eye out of curiosity.

"Amy sent you a birthday present. Here it is—happy fourth birthday!" And with that, Louie opened a box that contained the traditional carrot cake that Amy had given him each year for his birthday.

Twoey felt like it was the best birthday present in the world. Amy remembered, even if they were miles apart! It was so good to see the familiarly shaped carrot cake. Louie left so Twoey could enjoy his birthday present.

"Hey, Kidd!" Twoey shouted. "Breakfast for two! And it's from Amy." Kidd was suddenly awake and definitely hungry.

* * * *

Twoey was awakened early the next day to begin a new round of intense training.

"You're going for a big one this time," Louie told him.

"You've got to run your best for a longer distance, a mile-and-an-eighth."

Since Louie seemed to be concerned about the upcoming race, Twoey looked concerned.

Louie noticed the apprehension in Twoey and said, "Don't worry, Twoey, we'll get you up to the task. You'll be able to do it if you're in top condition. And it's my job to get you there."

Twoey worked hard on his speed and endurance. He ate the proper foods, obeyed Louie's commands, and trained with all the intensity of a top athlete, which he was.

But there would be many more surprises connected to this race.

A week before race day, Twoey and Kidd were loaded into their horse van. Each settled into his traveling routine. Kidd promptly curled up and fell asleep, while Twoey looked out the window at the scenery and let the wind blow over him. The trip seemed to be over before it started. They hadn't traveled very far at all.

When Twoey looked out, he didn't see the familiar sights associated with a racetrack.

"C'mon, Twoey. Wake up, Kidd!" Louie shouted with a laugh as he opened the van doors. "You're going on a brand new adventure today. You're going to take your first airplane ride."

"What's an airplane?" Kidd asked Twoey. Since Twoey had no idea how to answer him, he just said, "I don't know, but it sounds like fun." He hoped he was right.

Louie led Twoey and Kidd up a ramp into a big jet plane. Inside, the plane was designed like a barn with horse stalls complete with bedding. Twoey noticed he wasn't the only horse being loaded into this strange barn that Louie called an airplane.

"You'll be just fine here," Louie said as he closed the stall door. "You'll feel like you're being lifted up when the plane takes off and gets airborne. After that, the ride will be a lot smoother than your van ride. In a couple of hours, we'll be in California. Then another short van ride and you'll get to relax in your stall at the Santa Anita Race Track. We'll feed you a good dinner and you can settle in for the night. Okay, Twoey?" Louie asked, after explaining the routine.

Twoey nodded his head, as he always did when agreeing with Louie. He didn't really know all that he was agreeing to. The only familiar words he heard were van, relax, stall, and dinner.

Once the horses were locked in their stalls, none of them talked to each other. Each seemed to be nervous about the airplane trip. When Twoey realized he wasn't the only horse a little scared about what to expect from his first airplane ride, he actually calmed down a bit.

"What an adventure we're going to have, Kidd," Twoey said excitedly to his little friend, who was standing so close to him that Twoey could feel his legs shaking. "Hey, you're not scared, are you?" Twoey challenged. "What happened to you wanting to experience new things and explore new places?"

Kidd looked up at Twoey as if he had lost his mind. "Are you crazy?" Kidd yelled. "Didn't you hear what Louie said? 'When the plane takes off and gets airborne!' This thing leaves the ground!" Kidd shouted. "Don't you get it? We go up in the air. How can we do that? What keeps this barn in the air?"

Twoey didn't have the answer. But he did have confidence. "Think about it, Kidd. See all these other thoroughbreds? These are all very good racehorses that win a lot of money for their owners. Mr. Maxwell and the other owners would not put any of us in danger. I'm certain it's perfectly safe." He looked around his stall. "Besides, I trust Louie to take care of us. He'd never bring us here if it wasn't okay," Twoey said reassuringly.

"He said we're going to California," Twoey continued. "That must be pretty far away. I know you'd complain the whole trip if you had to spend several days in a horse van."

"Yeah, you're right," Kidd admitted. "Plus, think of all the bumps and bruises I might have gotten, not to mention the loss of sleep. I just can't sleep in those vans."

At that, Twoey let out a big laugh. "You, not sleep? You can sleep anywhere, anytime, and all day and all night!"

"What about you?" Kidd teased. "You can sleep standing up."

"Yeah, but I'm not going to sleep on this trip. I don't want to miss one minute of my first plane ride, which I think is about to begin."

The plane's engines began to roar. As the plane picked up speed, Twoey felt a feeling of being lifted, just like Louie predicted. It was a nice feeling. Even though he could hear the airplane engines, the ride was smooth, without the bumps and jolts he had become used to in his horse van.

"So," Twoey looked down at Kidd, "what do you think?"

"What!" Kidd replied. "You mean that was it?"

"Yeah, pretty smooth isn't it?" Twoey said.

"Well, with all the buildup of a first airplane ride, there wasn't much to it," Kidd complained, trying not to show how relieved he was. "Now that the excitement, as little as it was, is over, I think I'll lay down for a little snooze."

Twoey looked around at the other thoroughbreds and noticed that some were still looking nervous, especially a filly who looked about his age. Twoey spoke to her to reassure her. "You must be going to California to race?"

"Yes, I am," the filly responded. "I've never been there before. Have you?"

"No. In fact, this is my first plane ride. It's pretty neat, isn't it?" Twoey said with excitement.

"I guess so. I was pretty scared when we left the ground. It's hard to relax and enjoy the ride when you're scared," she admitted.

"Well, no need to be frightened anymore," Twoey assured her. "What's your name?"

"Contessa Star," she answered. "What's yours?"

"They call me Twoey," he replied, hoping she wouldn't laugh.

"What a nice name," she said.

"Do you really think so?" Twoey asked, surprised. "It's not a fancy name. Not like your name, Contessa Star. That's a great name."

"It's a name that's hard to live up to. So much is expected of me. It's a burden knowing that I'm not allowed to make a mistake. It's been very difficult trying to please every owner who expects me to win every race. I don't know how long I can continue to make them happy," she said, with a little fear in her voice.

"How many owners have you had?" Twoey asked.

"This last one makes five," she answered.

"But you're not very old." Twoey couldn't imagine having so many owners. "I think we're about the same age, aren't we? Four?" Twoey guessed.

"Yes, I'm four, but I've lived on five different farms in different states with different owners. Each new one enters me in higher paying races with a more competitive field and expects me to win a lot of money. I've been successful so far, but I know that there will come a day when I don't win. I don't know what will happen then. So much is expected of me," she said with sadness.

She looked at Twoey. "I wish I could be more like you,

Twoey. You obviously look forward to racing in California while I am dreading it."

"But Contessa, racing is in your blood and in your heart. You've been paying too much attention to what you think is expected of you." He thought of Diamond Knight's advice and decided to share it. "A real, veteran champion once told me 'Don't think too much. Pay attention to what's in your heart.'" He added some advice of his own. "We all train hard to be physically able to win our races, but we win with our hearts perhaps even more than our legs and strength."

Contessa looked at Twoey with admiration. "You're very smart, Twoey. And you're right. I have been so worried about what is expected of me because of my name and pedigree that I forgot who I am inside. I am a thoroughbred, a descendant of some of the greatest thoroughbreds in the world. You've given me back something I had lost. I had lost my will to win because I was too afraid of losing. Thank you, Twoey."

Twoey felt a little proud of himself and welcomed Contessa's compliment and her attention. "Where are you racing in California?" Twoey asked.

"Santa Anita Race Track. I race in a couple of days. I'm entered in the Santa Monica Handicap for fillies and mares four years old and older."

She explained more. "It's a seven-furlong race, and so it's not going to take a lot of stamina to win it, not like a mile or more. But I'll have to out-maneuver the other horses to be in the lead at the finish line," Contessa explained.

Twoey was surprised at her knowledge and wanted to know more. "Wow, you approach racing using a different kind of strategy. That's quite a talent," Twoey said admiringly.

"Well, in some races I know I'm not the fastest," Contessa admitted, "so I have to use strategy to be able to take the lead. For example, if I can sprint to the lead out of the gate and force the other horses to fall in behind me, I may slow down the pace to a speed that's comfortable for me. After the last turn, when the horses behind me try to pass me, I'll have the speed I need to stay in the lead." She said it as if she thought every thoroughbred knew that. "You must have a racing strategy, Twoey? What is it?"

"Oh, I just run as fast as I can right out of the gate, get in the lead, and keep running until the race is over," he laughed. He thought that was every thoroughbred's strategy. "I lost once and, believe me, it's no fun. You have mud and dirt in your eyes, your hair, and you're a real mess. I decided, after that loss, I would work as hard as I can to be the fastest and be able to run the longest so I wouldn't be humiliated like that again."

Contessa laughed at his honesty. "Where are you racing in California, Twoey?"

"Same place you are, Santa Anita. But my race is more than a week away. It's called the Strub Stakes for four-year-old thoroughbreds. It's long—a mile-and-an-eighth. No doubt I'll have a lot of work to do once we get there. But I have a nice owner and a great trainer."

"Hey, I'm entered in the Strub Stakes, too," a stallion called out after listening to the chatter between Twoey and Contessa. His impression of Twoey was that he was meek and timid—just a scared little colt he could intimidate.

"My name's Mountain Man and, Twoey, I suggest you don't challenge the Mountain on race day," he threatened.

Twoey didn't want to start a yelling match. He was familiar with the big egos of some thoroughbreds, and he had heard the threats before. He knew the best thing he could do was to ignore this new one.

He quietly called to Contessa and said, "Good luck. I know you'll win. Maybe we'll see each other again some day."

"I hope so, Twoey. I've really enjoyed talking to you. You've made the trip much easier," Contessa whispered back. "Good luck to you."

Soon the plane touched down in California and Twoey was ready to begin yet another new adventure.

First, though, he had to wake up Kidd who had slept through the whole flight.

CHAPTER NINETEEN

California Dreaming

Twoey and Kidd thought California was a good place to visit, with lots of trees and green pastures, and Twoey enjoyed good workout areas. He felt totally prepared by race day.

Because he trained very hard, he didn't have much time to spend with Kidd. At night, Kidd would tell him about all the places he had explored, so that Twoey could share Kidd's adventures even if he couldn't actually experience them.

Race day at Santa Anita arrived very quickly. Once he was in the gate, Twoey worked on his mental preparation—totally focused on the course in front of him. He visualized how his legs would run at great speed and how his body would feel weightless as the finish line got closer.

"And, they're off!" the track announcer shouted into the microphone as the gates flew open.

Twoey took the lead immediately and stayed on the rail, knowing that was the shortest distance to the finish line. Some horses tried to go around him, but every time they caught up to his back legs, Twoey found more energy and outran them, always staying in the lead. He kept running as fast as he could. His legs felt tired, his heart was beating very fast, and his breathing was hard, but he ignored the feelings and focused on the finish line. It was just ahead. He kept telling himself, "I can do it. I can do it. Just a little longer. Just a little faster."

Finally, his jockey began to slow him down. Twoey allowed himself to listen to the crowd cheering, to feel the jockey patting his neck in congratulations. Now he could relax and walk into the winner's circle where Mr. Maxwell and Louie would be waiting for him, smiling at him, patting him with affection.

There was no other feeling like it in the world, but Twoey also looked forward to the feeling of accomplishment that would come later as he shared the victory with Kidd. He would be groomed and fed for the night, and then he and Kidd could talk about all the events of the day as they rested in their stall.

As Twoey was being led into the winner's circle, Mountain Man walked by him. Instead of congratulating Twoey as some of the other thoroughbreds had, he threatened him: "Enjoy this one, because I'm going to make sure it's your last one. Remember the Mountain."

Twoey was tempted to answer him by saying something nasty, but instead he said, "You had a good run, Mountain Man. I look forward to our next race." Then Twoey stepped into the winner's circle where Louie and Mr. Maxwell held a large trophy and a check for $500,000. The cameras flashed and the crowd cheered as he took his place in the circle.

* * * *

At the J.R. Brand Ranch, Amy read every word of the article about Twoey's win at Santa Anita. She stared at his pictures in the paper. One showed him crossing the finish line, practically in a blur, and the other was Twoey in the winner's circle. He held his head up so high and looked so proud. Looking closer, she thought she could even see him smiling.

"Twoey, just look at you," Amy said, smiling with pride at

the picture. She took her scissors, clipped out the article and taped it in a scrapbook that was filled with pictures, ribbons, awards, letters, and articles about Twoey.

"Some day I'll show you this scrapbook, Twoey. Some day." Amy put the scrapbook next to her list of steps she needed to take in order to reach her goals. She was beginning to put checkmarks by some of the steps. Each checkmark meant she was getting closer to her ultimate goal and closer to being reunited with Twoey.

* * * *

Twoey learned that he would be staying at Santa Anita for a while longer to compete in other high-stakes races. His next competition was in just two weeks. It was a mile-and-a-half race for four year olds and older. Most of the same horses in the Strub Stakes would be competing in this one, too, including Mountain Man.

Twoey prepared himself as much as he could for his second race. He knew this race could be even tougher to win because the horses and jockeys had seen his racing strategy and they would be anxious to try to beat him.

As the race started and the thoroughbreds raced down the track, Twoey and Mountain Man were pretty evenly matched. Twoey stayed next to the rail, forcing Mountain Man to run on the outside, making him run farther. Twoey realized now what Contessa had meant when she talked about strategy. He had to use strategy to keep Mountain Man on the outside of him in order to stay ahead of him.

Twoey won the race but defeated Mountain Man by only a head. It was his closest race ever.

Twoey talked with Kidd that night in their stall. "It seems like every race is getting harder to win. I am running as fast as I can, and after I pass the last turn, I think my legs can't run any more. But then I see the finish line just ahead and my heart seems to get bigger and my legs seem to go faster." He remembered every moment of the race. "Trouble is, many of the other horses seem to pick up speed, too, in the final stretch."

Kidd knew that Twoey was training and working as hard as he ever had. He tried to encourage him. "You seem to always manage to cross the finish line first, though, so you're doing something right."

Twoey appreciated Kidd's support. "Well, so far, so good."

As Twoey settled in for sleep that night, he kept replaying the race. When dreams filled his mind, he saw the inside rail of the racetrack rushing by him in a blur. On his right side, he saw an enormous thoroughbred come up beside him. The big thoroughbred's nostrils were flaring, his mouth was open. As he passed Twoey, he laughed.

CHAPTER TWENTY

Revenge

The biggest race of the year at Santa Anita was in just two weeks. The Santa Anita Handicap, for a million dollars, was a mile-and-a-quarter race. Again, the same competitors were entered, with long shots added to the race. Their owners hoped against the odds they could win in an upset over the favorites.

Louie assured Twoey he could take the lead and keep it if he stayed on the rail and ran at his fastest pace. Twoey felt that he could handle it. He was in terrific physical shape and was mentally confident.

At the starting gate, the horses were tense, waiting for the race to begin. They had picked up on the tension of their owners and trainers. Everyone wanted to be in the winner's circle after the race, accepting the million-dollar check and receiving the prominence in the racing world that this victory would bring them.

When the bell rang, the gates flew open and Twoey sprinted to the rail, ahead of the others. Mountain Man was behind him on the rail. Twoey didn't want to follow the strategy of slowing the pace. He felt if he could keep the pace at his fastest speed, Mountain Man would not be able to keep up. The two raced at top speed, leaving the field of other thoroughbreds behind. Twoey and Mountain Man were flying down the track running stride-for-stride.

The crowd could not believe the speed of the two champions. They watched in awe as the two competitors broke speed records at every turn. In the final stretch to the finish line, Twoey still had a slight lead, but Mountain Man was right on his back hooves.

Suddenly, Twoey felt a horrible pain in his right rear leg. He almost stumbled but managed to immediately get back into the rhythm of his run. Mountain Man, with a mighty effort, tried to go around him, but Twoey pushed with all his heart and energy. With a final spurt, Twoey finished a nose ahead of Mountain Man to win the biggest race of his life.

As soon as he crossed the finish line, the terrible pain in his leg overcame Twoey. He had never been injured, never experienced pain. He didn't understand what was happening. He felt like his leg was going to give out. He began limping, afraid that he would fall if he put all his weight on that leg. His jockey immediately slowed him and got off to examine his hind leg. It was bleeding from a deep gouge.

Mr. Maxwell and Louie had seen what had happened. They tried to get through the crowd in the stands to get to Twoey on the track and see how badly he was hurt. They raced to Twoey, forgetting about the million-dollar check waiting for them in the winner's circle.

"He's got a pretty deep gouge in the back of that right leg," the jockey said.

Louie was examining Twoey's leg and shaking his head. "I saw that horse do it deliberately," he said. "Mountain Man intended to injure Twoey because Twoey kept beating him."

"You don't think it was an accident that Mountain Man's front hoof ripped into Twoey's back leg?" Mr. Maxwell asked.

"That was no accident," Louie accused. "Through binoculars I kept watching Mountain Man try to get closer and closer to Twoey's back legs. He even tried to slice his leg earlier in the race, but Twoey was too far in front. He finally got close enough to kick out his front hoof at Twoey's back leg. It's a wonder Twoey didn't fall right there. He could have been killed."

Louis shook his head in disbelief at Twoey's injury. "That Mountain Man is just plain mean, and the jockey is just as much to blame. He could have pulled him back."

"You know that's not going to happen in a million-dollar race, Louie," Mr. Maxwell said knowingly as he stroked Twoey's neck, trying to comfort him.

"Mountain Man and his jockey were out to win at any cost, even by hurting Twoey. Well, I'm not going to let them get away with it," Mr. Maxwell promised. "I'm going to have the racing commissioner look carefully at the race video and then I'm filing a grievance against Mountain Man and his jockey."

The jockey said, "I'll file an objection, too. Maybe we can get them off this racing circuit." Mr. Maxwell and the jockey continued discussing what action they could take.

Louie patted Twoey's neck and looked him in the eye. He softly said to him, "I didn't realize what a great champion you really are, Twoey. I mean, I knew you could run like the wind and win your races, but you showed everybody today that you have the heart of a champion. You overcame a tremendous obstacle that should have stopped you, but you wouldn't let it. I have renewed respect and admiration for you, Twoey." Then Louie gave Twoey a little bow as if he were honoring royalty.

"Do you think he's up to making an appearance in the winner's circle?" Mr. Maxwell asked of the jockey and Louie.

"He did everything he could to win that race, didn't he? He's earned the right to be in the winner's circle to receive all the glory he deserves," Louie answered. "In fact, I'm not sure you could keep him out. It's part of his racing tradition, you know. He always finishes a race in the winner's circle."

"Well, let's not spoil it for him this time." Smiling, the trainer, the jockey, and the owner all walked slowly while Twoey limped to the winner's circle. As Twoey was being praised and photographed in the winner's circle, Mr. Maxwell was accepting the million-dollar check.

But Louie couldn't smile for very long. As soon as the pictures were over, he let his concern show on his face. He couldn't help but wonder if this would be Twoey's last time in the winner's circle. Louie felt that Twoey's leg would heal, but he was concerned that the memory of the pain might affect Twoey emotionally. If Twoey were to enter the winner's circle again, he would have to heal his mind. Louie knew from experience that sometimes was more difficult than healing an injury.

CHAPTER TWENTY-ONE

Healing

Twoey did not go back to his stall. He was taken directly to a veterinary hospital for a complete examination and x-rays. As doctors and nurses led him from one room to another and moved him this way and that, Twoey was surprised that he was not afraid. The pain in his leg seemed to overshadow any other feelings, even fear. He would have to stay overnight for evaluation.

Kidd was frantic with worry. It was getting dark and Twoey had not returned to the barn. He had looked all over Santa Anita for him. He had long ago stopped going to the track during Twoey's races. Now that they were traveling all over the country, Kidd had new territory to explore, trouble to find, and generally only a few days to do it in before they were off to a new location.

Each night, Kidd would tell Twoey stories about his adventures that day. Kidd knew Twoey loved hearing the stories. Although Twoey was always training or racing, whenever Kidd told him all the elaborate details of his day, Twoey felt he was right there with him, sharing his adventures. Kind of like being in two places at the same time.

With nowhere else to look for Twoey, Kidd returned to the stall to wait. He heard Louie's footsteps and cried out in lonely alarm, trying to ask why Twoey hadn't come home.

"It's going to be okay, Kidd," Louie tried to reassure the little goat as he knelt down in Twoey's stall. "Twoey had an accident," Louie explained. "He's in the hospital now. I wish I could make you understand, but I'm afraid I don't even understand."

Kidd could sense the fear and sadness in Louie's voice, and he became even more alarmed.

"Here's some food, Kidd. Get some sleep. Your buddy should be back tomorrow, then we'll just have to see where we stand." Then Louie slowly walked out of Twoey's stall with his head down, looking as if he had lost his best friend.

Kidd couldn't eat or sleep. He had always been able to eat anything and sleep anywhere, but not tonight. He couldn't believe that Twoey was hurt. He would rest and think of ways he could help Twoey get well again.

* * * * *

When Twoey woke up, he didn't know where he was, but he knew he wasn't in his stall at Santa Anita. He looked at his aching hind leg and saw that it was bandaged. With a grimace, he remembered hurting his leg on the racetrack. He heard the familiar voices of Louie and Mr. Maxwell talking to someone in front of the stall. He pawed at the ground and whinnied to get their attention.

"You're awake," Louie said, smiling at him. "The doctor says you're a very good patient and you're going to be okay. Isn't that good news, Twoey? You can go home!"

Twoey nodded and whinnied even louder. The doctor, Louie, and Mr. Maxwell all laughed. Twoey wasn't sure where he was, but he knew he wanted to go home and see Kidd.

Twoey walked out of the hospital with a limp. He tried to keep his weight off his bandaged hind leg. On the way home, he heard Louie talk to him about hydrotherapy and whirlpools to help strengthen his leg, but he didn't understand what he was talking about. He was so tired and his leg ached. He couldn't concentrate on what Louie was saying. He just wanted to rest in his stall, talk to Kidd, and eat some dinner before going to sleep again.

Kidd's joyful welcome made Twoey feel a good deal better. Being back home with Kidd even took away some of his pain and fear. As his anxiety left, he suddenly felt too tired to eat or even talk. Kidd urged him to get some sleep and said they had plenty of time to talk later. Kidd even promised not to eat all the food.

Instead of sleeping in his usual corner location, Kidd settled by the stall door, feeling the need to protect Twoey and make sure no one came to hurt him or take him away.

* * * *

Louie hated having the conversation with Mr. Maxwell, but he had to tell him the facts. "I'm afraid we can't keep him here, Mr. Maxwell," Louie was explaining. "Twoey can't race at Santa Anita anymore this season. He needs physical therapy, rest, and rehabilitation. It's not only the right hind leg that is injured from being cut down by Mountain Man. He's also lame on his left front leg. The vet figures he injured it in the last spurt to the finish line when he probably shifted his weight off his injured right hind leg."

Louie did not want to make the next suggestion, but felt in was in the best interest of Twoey and Mr. Maxwell's entire stable of racehorses. "We're entering our busiest racing season, with meets all over the country, and we just can't take him with us. It's not in Twoey's best interest."

Louie explained that he had made arrangements for Twoey to stay in California at an equine health and rehabilitation center. There, Twoey would receive the medical attention he needed, the physical therapy necessary to bring him back up to speed, and the relaxation that his body and mind now required in order to heal.

"You're sure that this is the best decision for Twoey?" Mr. Maxwell asked.

"I'm afraid it's about the only decision we can make," Louie answered. "I'm assured it's an excellent facility. He'll need months to recuperate and then he'll have to retrain. As much as Twoey means to both of us, we have to be honest. We just can't give him all the attention he's going to need. We have a full race schedule with ten other good racing prospects. We can't cancel our racing season to concentrate on one horse, even if it is Twoey, our best thoroughbred."

"You're right, of course," Mr. Maxwell reluctantly agreed. "This racing business is a business, after all. Sometimes I tend to forget that." He hated the fact that the decision had to be made to leave Twoey behind in California, but he was at least determined to make Twoey's stay comfortable for the horse. "Make sure Twoey gets the best care and also make sure that he's not separated from Kidd," Mr. Maxwell demanded.

"I know Twoey well enough by now to know that he'd be lost without that little goat," Louie agreed.

"They are quite a pair," Mr. Maxwell laughed, "and an inseparable pair. That's one thing I won't change—Kidd goes with Twoey."

The next morning, Twoey and Kidd were loaded into a horse van by Louie. With tears in his eyes, he said to them, "I'm sorry we can't take you with us. You get some rest and get healthy again."

Then Louie patted Kidd's head and said, "You make sure he follows doctor's orders and, Kidd, look after him. He's very special to all of us."

* * * *

Twoey and Kidd tried to settle into the van but it was impossible. Twoey's leg still hurt and the bandage was uncomfortable. He was tired and hungry, even though he knew he couldn't eat. He didn't understand where they were going or what they would face when they got there. He only knew that Louie and Mr. Maxwell were not going with them. Twoey closed his eyes and let his mind wander through comforting memories.

As the sun beamed into the windows of the van and the wind blew over Twoey's body, he relaxed and began dreaming. He had been afraid the very first time he had gotten into the horse van, but the sun and wind coming in the windows had calmed him. He remembered seeing the trees, green pastures, and fields as they sped past in a blur. He had felt the wind as it seemed to stroke his head, neck, and back in a gentle caress that silently told him he would be all right.

Twoey awakened slightly when the van jiggled as it went over some bumps in the road. He looked out and saw a sea of cars and trucks speeding past them. The scenery wasn't green as it was in his dream, but the wind coming in the windows felt the same. He closed his eyes again to remember.

* * * *

At the J.R. Brand Ranch, Amy read again the California newspaper article about Twoey and the Santa Anita million-dollar race. She looked closely at the winner's-circle picture of Twoey, Louie, the jockey, and Mr. Maxwell. They were all smiling. Nothing in the picture indicated that something was wrong.

Amy's dad had received a telephone call from Louie. Amy could tell from overhearing her dad's end of the conversation that it was about Twoey. She caught snatches about the Racing Commissioner being alerted and a grievance being filed. "But why?" she wondered. "What did that have to do with Twoey?" She reasoned Louie would call her dad only if it had to do with Twoey. She knew that even if it was bad news, her dad would tell her as soon as he got off the phone.

Amy looked at the winning picture again as she sat at her study desk in her bedroom. "He won a million-dollar race," Amy whispered. "That's good news, not bad. If Louie called with good news, dad would tell me immediately." She suddenly put the picture down. "But he didn't tell me immediately." Amy said it with the realization that she would soon hear bad news about Twoey.

Amy cut out the pictures and the article and placed them in Twoey's scrapbook. Then her dad knocked on her door.

CHAPTER TWENTY-TWO

Coach Kidd

Twoey and Kidd stayed in California for several months. As part of his physical therapy, Twoey would stand in buckets of ice to help keep down the swelling in his injured legs. He was allowed to rest in his stall and then he would be taken to a swimming pool with whirling water that felt so good on his entire body. It was his favorite part of therapy.

Kidd was at his side wherever he went. Kidd once even dipped his front hoof into the swimming pool just to test it, but he refused to get any more of himself wet.

One day they were led out to a pasture. They were the only ones there. The sun was shining to warm their bodies, yet there was a breeze to cool them and shade trees to lie down underneath. Kidd was stretched out on the grass when he looked up and said to Twoey, "We must be very rich. This is like heaven for horses. You get pampered day and night, we have the best food to eat, and just look at this place." Kidd looked around to admire the view. "This is paradise," Kidd smiled with contentment. "Maybe we can stay here forever." Kidd closed his eyes ready to dream of a perfect future.

"I don't want to stay here forever!" Twoey exclaimed with a hint of anger in his voice. "In fact, I wish we never had to come here." Twoey jumped up and began pacing in front of

Kidd. "I want to go home to be with Louie. I want to get back into training. I want to race!" Twoey said in frustration.

He stopped pacing, hung his head, and gave a sigh of defeat. "I haven't trained in so long that it's going to take me a long time to get back into racing form."

Kidd stared at Twoey, shocked by what he was hearing.

Twoey continued, talking to himself more than to Kidd. "My legs feel strong again. I feel healthy but I'm getting too much rest. I need to get back to work," Twoey said with frustration.

Kidd wanted to close his eyes again and rewind the last few seconds to the moment before when he and Twoey were laying in the grass taking a nap, enjoying the luxury surrounding them. Kidd thought to himself, "Why can't things just stay the same for a while? Why do things have to keep changing?" But Kidd knew Twoey needed him, so he got up. "Well, what are you waiting for then?" Kidd snapped at Twoey.

Twoey looked a little shocked at Kidd's sudden outburst. "Well, I'm waiting for a trainer to work with me and show me what to do," Twoey answered, surprised at Kidd's gruffness.

"As if you don't know what to do," Kidd said. "You've been training all your life. You must have some idea how to get started again."

Twoey looked at Kidd as if he were crazy. Do it himself? Without a trainer? Kidd didn't know what he was talking about. But Kidd's comments had Twoey thinking.

"C'mon," Kidd urged. "First thing, let's walk around this entire pasture. Then, while I watch you, you can trot around the pasture. If your legs aren't bothering you, we'll do more. Or, I should say, you'll do more."

Twoey looked at Kidd. "Do you really think I can train myself?"

Kidd laughed. "Are you kidding? You are the one who was doing all the training, not the trainers. They only told you what to do. You did it." Now that Kidd had Twoey's attention, he challenged him. "All those hours, weeks, and months of training, didn't you learn anything?"

A challenge was exactly what Twoey needed. Off they went, the champion thoroughbred and his new coach and trainer, Kidd the goat.

* * * *

Twoey and Kidd kept up their training routine every time they were in the pasture. Twoey first walked around the pasture as a kind of warm-up, to strengthen his leg. Then, he would begin a slow trot, and he was finally able to gallop at a pretty good pace, even if it wasn't on a racetrack or training track.

His workouts in the pasture did not go unnoticed.

"Well, will you look at that?" a handler at the equine center observed as he looked out over the pasture. "That thoroughbred is doing his own training." He could hardly believe what he was seeing.

Twoey was not just playing around, he was galloping and running as if he were training for a race.

"Well, don't that beat all," the handler said, shaking his head in disbelief. "I better tell the vet."

"You mean to tell me that Twoey has been training on his own?" Louie asked the vet with amazement.

"It's the strangest sight I've even seen," the vet replied. "That little goat acts like he's a coach. He watches Twoey as he walks, then trots, then gallops around the pasture."

The vet laughed. "If Twoey's willing to train on his own to get back to racing, I'd say he's ready to go home."

CHAPTER TWENTY-THREE

Back on Track

Soon Twoey was back in real training again—back home with Louie. His speed and endurance were improving, and he was physically ready to compete again. Kidd had been working on his confidence, so he also felt mentally prepared.

"Think we're going to see how you do at Belmont in New York," Louie informed Twoey. "I think you're ready for the seven-furlong Vosburgh Race. I don't want to put you in a mile race yet. Let's test your speed, then we'll go after endurance."

Kidd, who felt he had become Twoey's coach, agreed with the trainer's strategy and told Twoey, "He's smart to enter you in these shorter races first. It's kind of like you're training for the longer ones. You have to work up to them gradually."

* * * *

At the end of September, six months after his injury, Twoey stepped into the starting gate at Belmont. He loved it. He felt so alive. He was back. He sprinted out and headed for the rail, in his usual racing strategy. He quickly realized that it was going to be a difficult race.

Before his injury, speed and winning came naturally to him. Now he had to work very, very hard. He was putting demands on his muscles, trying to get his body to remember the rhythm of running fast. His mind knew what to do. Now if he could only get his body to obey his mind. He ignored the aches in his legs and the tiredness in his body as he kept running. He wondered, "How much farther is it to the finish line?"

He was focusing so much on his own race that he didn't even realize some horses were passing him. He just wanted to get to the finish line.

Back in his stall, Twoey told Kidd he didn't feel like talking about the race. The handlers had rubbed down his sore muscles but they still ached. He knew that they would heal soon, but he wondered how long it would take to heal the ache in his heart.

He had tried his best to win, but it hadn't been enough. He hated to disappoint everyone, but their disappointment was nothing compared with the frustration Twoey felt with himself.

Kidd knew there was nothing he could say to ease Twoey's distress, so he let Twoey try to think it out himself.

* * * *

The next morning, Twoey awoke with the competitive sparkle back in his eyes, and he was anxious to get to the training track. When he saw Louie walking toward his stall, he let out the loudest whinny to let Louie know he was ready to get to work.

He had only two weeks to prepare for the next race. He approached it as a brand new challenge, a new beginning.

At the end of his second race at Belmont, Twoey didn't cross the finish line first, but he was within feet of winning, coming in second. He and Louie felt good about his performance in the race. Twoey felt he was finally getting back on track.

In his third race, two weeks later, Twoey and another horse were running side-by-side, stride-for-stride, to a photo finish. Twoey came up short by a nose, but it was his best showing thus far.

Louie felt Twoey was improving his speed and endurance and was ready again to compete in a longer race at Aqueduct Racetrack. The Cigar Mile race was for $350,000, and he had less than a month to prepare.

* * * *

As they left the horse van at Aqueduct, Twoey and Kidd immediately heard the loud noises of the city and the roar of airplanes flying overhead. Aqueduct was located in New York City, where the sounds of bells, horns, and people shouting or laughing are constant. Twoey tried to concentrate on his last-minute training, but he was finding it hard to focus.

In the starting gate, waiting for the other horses to be loaded and the bell to ring, Twoey remembered Diamond Knight talking about Aqueduct Racetrack and how he had to be especially focused on the race. Twoey's next thought was like a bolt of lightning to his heart—it was at this track that Diamond Knight was critically injured two years ago!

When the bell rang and the gates flew open, Twoey couldn't move. His jockey put the whip to him to wake him from his trance, and Twoey finally bolted out of the gate. The other horses were so far ahead of him that he knew he could not catch them. He had failed again.

Louie came to his stall that night. "I wish I knew what was going on in your head, Twoey. You never balked at the gate before."

Twoey wished he could tell him about Diamond Knight and the sudden fear that overtook him. He wished he could convince him that it would never happen again.

Louie put his arms around Twoey's neck. "You were one of the best thoroughbreds I have ever trained. We really were quite a team, weren't we? I doubt I'll ever have another one like you." Louie held onto Twoey's neck and felt his eyes fill with tears. He said with sadness and remorse, "I'm sorry I let you down." Then Louie let go and walked out of the stall.

* * * *

Louie didn't train Twoey for several weeks. Then, he suddenly showed up with a smile on his face.

Someone carrying a box was walking behind him. With tears of happiness streaming down her face, Amy stepped out from behind Louie.

Twoey whinnied and shook his head from side-to-side, as if to say, "Yes, yes, yes. It's really you!" It was Twoey's fifth birthday and Amy had not forgotten him.

After lengthy hugs, Amy opened the box. "Here's your carrot cake, Twoey." She set it down and looked up at him. "We've both reached a milestone. You're five and I'm eighteen. I'll be going to college soon."

Twoey looked closely at Amy and saw that she had changed. She was no longer the little girl with the school backpack. She was a young woman. But one thing had not changed. In her eyes, he saw her deep love for him. That meant more to him than he expected.

He had changed, too. He was no longer the best, the champion thoroughbred. He was trying very hard to get back what he had lost, but the realization that she loved him even now—when he was not the best—gave him courage to keep trying.

"I wish I could stay longer, Twoey. I had to come see you, even if just for a few moments. Someday..." Amy stopped when she said the word that had become a promise to both of them. "Someday," she continued, "I'll get to stay longer." She gave him another big hug, then turned and slowly walked away.

CHAPTER TWENTY-FOUR

The Cost of Winning

The following day, Louie began talking to Twoey with enthusiasm. "I think Mr. Maxwell and I have made a decision that will make you happy." Louie hoped he was right.

"You're a great competitor, Twoey, and it's not fair for you to compete in races that may be above your ability now. You're a winner and that's where you belong, in the winner's circle."

Twoey lowered his head and tried to understand what Louie was telling him. He agreed that he wanted to be in the winner's circle.

"At first, you and Kidd will be sad to leave. I know I will miss you both. But after you start winning again, I know the happiness will return."

Twoey raised his head and looked at Louie.

Louie looked into the horse's eyes with admiration as he said, "You're a champion. You have the competitive spirit and the heart to win. We're going to give you every chance to be back on top."

Twoey liked hearing what Louie was saying. He missed the winner's circle. He missed being first across the finish line. He hated not being out in front.

He couldn't wait to show them that he could be number one again. He felt like kicking and whinnying and jumping for joy. Amy had come with his birthday carrot cake and showed him she still loved him and had not forgotten him. Louie was going to get him back in the winner's circle. He was now full of hope again. He was thinking and dreaming so much of the winner's circle that he didn't see Louie turn and leave.

Kidd, though, had listened more closely to what Louie had said. He didn't look up at Twoey. He kept munching on the last carrot from the carrot cake with his head down, pretending to concentrate on his treat. He didn't even look up when Louie left. Unlike Twoey, Kidd had heard and understood every word Louie had said.

"Hey, Kidd," Twoey said happily. "What a great year this is going to be. Didn't you hear Louie? We're going to be back in the winner's circle again."

Kidd didn't respond. He kept looking down, staring at the carrot. He had lost his appetite. His stomach felt like it was turning into knots.

"Hey, Buddy!" Twoey yelled, disappointed at Kidd's lack of interest. "Aren't you happy for me? Is that carrot more important than our future and happiness?"

Kidd kept pretending to munch on the carrot, knowing that what he had to say would shock Twoey.

"Fine!" Twoey shouted angrily. "Be that way! You know, you're turning into an old goat. You used to be a lot of fun. You used to care what happened to me."

Twoey was surprised when Kidd still said nothing. Usually Kidd would snap back with some clever remark whenever Twoey got angry. There was nothing but silence. When Twoey still didn't get a response from Kidd, he tried teasing him.

"Remember when we were young and Louie joked about you being the jockey, riding around on my back? Why don't we try that? Maybe that's what I need to get back in the winner's circle. Instead of my coach, you can be my jockey!" Twoey glanced to see if Kidd had heard him.

Kidd finally looked up. He couldn't keep the smile or the laughter from bubbling up. "That was when you were shorter," Kidd teased back. "Now look at you! I'd need a big ladder to get up on your back." Kidd laughed at the vision that was popping into his head. "I prefer it right here on the ground, thank you."

Twoey was happy that Kidd had snapped out of whatever mood he had been in. "Thank you. I thought for a minute you might never talk to me again," Twoey said, relieved.

Kidd thought as he looked at Twoey that, even though Twoey was a champion, he still sometimes acted like a youngster. Twoey always saw the positive side of things, always knew tomorrow would be better than today.

Kidd now feared 'tomorrow' after what Louie had said, but he would not talk to Twoey about it. No sense in both of them being afraid until there really was something to fear.

* * * *

The 'tomorrow' Kidd had feared arrived very soon. Suddenly Twoey understood what Louie had meant when he said Twoey would get back in the winner's circle. He meant it would be with a new owner, competing with thoroughbreds that were not the best in the country. With sad good-byes from Mr. Maxwell and Louie, Twoey and Kidd were loaded onto a trailer to go to their new home, new owner, and new trainer.

After many pep talks by Kidd, Twoey gave his new trainer all his attention and worked as hard as he could. Twoey thought back over his racing career and was confused. He was sold the first time because he was too good at winning and needed to compete in better races. Now he was sold because he wasn't good enough to compete in the top races and needed to race against horses he could beat.

He decided all he could do was race at his best all the time.

Twoey soon realized that the big races he competed in, with Louie as his trainer, felt no different in many ways to him than his current races. The importance of the race or the dollars it paid made no difference to how he raced. Once he was on the track racing to the finish line, his race was the only race that mattered, irregardless of how much money it paid the owner. It was still competition, which he loved, and he still had to perform to the best of his ability.

Twoey was a winner again! In the winner's circle, his new owner and trainer praised Twoey, just as he had been praised by Amy, and then Mr. Maxwell and Louie.

His new owner was very happy with him and his winning streak. He made money, although Twoey knew these races didn't pay as much as the high-money races. To make as much money as possible, the new owner raced Twoey more often. He had a shorter time to recuperate.

Twoey again earned the reputation of a champion as he won race after race.

* * * *

As he left the winner's circle following his most recent win, Twoey felt a stab of pain in his right front leg. He limped off the track and was taken to his stall.

Kidd took his role as Twoey's coach and caretaker seriously. He was always making sure that Twoey ate the right food, got rest, and was protected from intruders. Kidd slept by the stall door so he knew who was coming near Twoey.

When he saw Twoey limping into the stall, he was nervous for Twoey. He silently wondered if the trainer would send him away again for medical treatment and rehabilitation. If so, would Kidd get to go with him? Would he and Twoey have to start all over again with the training, just as they had done the last time?

"What happened? How badly are you hurt?" Kidd asked Twoey.

"My leg just started hurting after I won that last race," Twoey explained, in obvious pain. "It hurts when I try to stand on it."

"Well, then, stay off it," Kidd ordered. "Here, you rest. I'll bring some food over to you and, after you eat, try to get some sleep."

Sleep sounded very good to Twoey. He admitted that he enjoyed Kidd acting like a nurse sometimes. He was thankful for the attention, but most of all for the companionship.

The next morning, Twoey's leg was examined. "Let's give him some Bute," the trainer said to a handler. "It's an anti-inflammatory drug that should make him feel better. I want him ready to race again by the end of the week."

Twoey did feel better. Much of the pain was gone and, what pain remained, he could handle. But after he crossed the finish line, winning his next race, Twoey's leg hurt something awful. He again limped back to his stall.

"You've got to stop racing for awhile, Twoey," Kidd warned him. "Give that leg time to heal."

"There is no time, Kidd," Twoey admitted truthfully. "I've got to keep racing and I've got to keep winning or I'll be sold again." Twoey knew it was now a fact of his life.

Twoey saw the look of fear on Kidd's face and tried to reassure him. No sense in both of them being afraid. "Don't worry," Twoey laughed. "You know me, I always come out on top."

Twoey wanted to get Kidd's mind on something else. "Now what's for dinner? I'm as hungry as a horse!" And they both laughed.

Twoey couldn't sleep that night. He was much more worried about his injury than he wanted Kidd to know. He knew that somehow he would have to race even while his leg was hurting. He decided he would not think of the pain, but concentrate only on his race and his speed. He would automatically do what he was trained to do.

While Twoey tried to ignore the pain in his leg, he knew that his injury was getting worse each time he raced. He was given cortisone injections in his knee and then he felt no pain. Twoey was running as fast as he could, but he had lost the rhythm he always relied on to win every race. He realized that his injured leg took away his rhythm, and, as hard as he tried, he couldn't get it back.

CHAPTER TWENTY-FIVE

Today Is the Day

The day finally arrived that Twoey had dreaded but knew would come. Without a word from his owner or trainer, Twoey and Kidd were loaded into a van. He had been sold to another owner who was racing horses at less competitive tracks.

Twoey didn't do much training with the new owner or trainer. He just exercised.

His actual races became his training. He told himself that it didn't matter that he wasn't being pampered like he was when he lived with Amy or Louie. He tried to convince himself that he no longer needed the high-quality training. He knew what he was supposed to do. He had to concentrate on his race and run as fast as he could.

He still received a cortisone shot in his leg to take away the pain so he could race without stumbling.

His jockey would use the whip on him in every race to get him to go faster. Twoey had never been whipped before and he didn't like it. He thought they should know he always focused on the race and ran his best. They didn't have to whip him.

Even though Twoey tried to keep Kidd from knowing how much pain he was feeling, Kidd could see the pain in his eyes and the way he held his head. The sparkle was gone from Twoey's eyes.

Twoey knew that his sixth birthday had come and gone. He knew in his heart that Amy would not have forgotten him. He felt sure she couldn't find him to send his carrot cake. He smiled to himself and thought about how much the simple little cake had meant to them.

Twoey made himself stop remembering. The memories were too painful now. If he thought of the times when he was happiest, it made him realize even more just how sad he was now.

* * * *

It finally happened. Twoey had known this day would come but he just didn't know exactly when. As he made the final turn in a race where he was behind a couple of horses, Twoey fell. He could go no farther. He knew he could race no more. His leg had finally given out.

Twoey and Kidd were silent in their stall. They couldn't say anything to each other because they were too afraid of what was ahead of them. Twoey didn't know exactly what happened to thoroughbred racehorses when they couldn't race anymore.

He knew that Diamond Knight was doing well because Amy would make sure he was taken care of when he could no longer race. And Queenie, Twoey's mother, was with Diamond Knight.

But what would happen to him? And what would happen to Kidd? He couldn't think of the future, only the present. He looked at Kidd who was lying at the stall door looking forlorn.

Kidd was his best friend and had always been able to cheer up the horse when things were going wrong. It was now Twoey's turn to help take away Kidd's sadness.

"Hey, Buddy," Twoey said. "Look at the bright side. Now

that I don't race anymore we can spend more time together, go on adventures. And you don't have to see me with dirt all over my face ever again." Twoey noticed Kidd beginning to smile.

"I have to admit," Kidd said, with a little smile, "that will be an improvement." But his smile faded quickly and he asked, "We will be able to stay together, right, Twoey? Wherever they take you, please, please make them take me, too," Kidd pleaded.

Twoey tried to laugh and ease Kidd's fears. He promised the small goat, "You and I are a team. Nobody is going to separate us. If they try to take me away without you, I'll kick and scream and be uncontrollable."

Kidd felt better and added, "And that's what I'll do, too. They'll have quite a fight on their hands if they try to separate us!"

* * * *

No one bothered Twoey and Kidd. The handler at the horse farm came to their stall to deliver food but he never talked to them. He just left the food and silently walked away.

No one talked to them or came by to pat Twoey's head or stroke his neck. There were no hugs or treats. Twoey felt an emptiness. He realized with sadness that there was no one to love him here. He tried to convince himself that it didn't matter. He didn't need love. He felt he couldn't trust people as he had before coming here. "It's better to be alone," he decided.

If a stranger came up to the stall door, Twoey would kick and put his ears back as a sign that he was to be left alone.

Kidd would yell as loud as he could in his little goat's voice. It made Twoey silently smile when he did it, because he doubted Kidd scared anybody.

Kidd had heard stories about some of the thoroughbreds that could no longer race. Some thoroughbreds were sold at an auction. No one seemed to know what happened to them after that. He would never tell Twoey what he had heard. He would do what he could to protect Twoey.

* * * *

It seemed that every day at least one stranger would come to his stall to look at Twoey. The stranger would talk to Twoey's owner but would always walk away shaking their head. Twoey heard his owner say that he was worth more money than a couple hundred dollars. He'd tell the potential buyer that Twoey's injury wasn't serious, that Twoey just needed stall rest for about six months, and then he'd be as good as new.

Twoey knew that his leg was so badly damaged that he'd never race again. He was thankful he could even walk and credited his previous physical training for giving him the strength to walk.

Twoey thought about the money. Buyers were only offering a couple hundred dollars for him. Just a few years ago, he had won a million-dollar race. What did it mean? That he was basically worthless today? Although his body might be broken a bit, his heart was as big and willing to please and full of love to give as it always was. He was the same inside as he was when he was a champion. Why didn't someone see into his heart?

One day a woman stopped by his stall and started talking to him. It had been a long time since anyone actually paid any attention to him. Her voice was soft and he liked hearing it. She held out a carrot.

Twoey felt like a warm blanket had been pulled over him. Here was someone who treated him with kindness, someone who seemed to care about him. It had been so long since any-one had paid attention to him and given him a treat. Twoey gently took the carrot and, when he had eaten it, he nuzzled her hand.

"Well, aren't you the gentleman," the woman said and stroked his head.

Kidd was always on alert with strangers, but he sensed immediately that this woman would not harm Twoey, so he came closer, too.

"So you're Kidd," she said with a smile. "I brought a treat for you, too." She gave him a carrot. "I hear you're quite a pair—one won't go anyplace without the other."

Twoey nodded in agreement and Kidd let out a little sound to confirm her statement.

The woman with the soft voice and smiling face walked into his stall and continued to stroke Twoey's neck while looking at his body and legs. "You've got a very bad leg," she told him, and added, "but you're pretty strong to be able to stand on it."

She looked at Twoey's eyes with admiration. "You've got a lot of character and pride, Twoey. I can see you're a champion in your heart. You don't have to be on a racetrack to prove it."

She made Twoey feel good again. Kidd could see that a sparkle had returned to Twoey's eyes. Kidd realized how love and attention could make such a difference. Twoey looked proud again and full of hope.

The kind woman walked away, and Twoey stuck his head out of his stall so he could watch her. She talked with his owner. Twoey could hear her explaining that she was with a thoroughbred placement organization named CANTER.

"CANTER finds new homes for thoroughbreds that must leave the life of racing," she explained to the owner. "We can find a new, loving home for Twoey where he will be happy and healthy."

Twoey saw the woman and his owner shake hands. She returned to Twoey's stall with a big smile on her face.

"You're going to a new life, Twoey," she told him, and then she looked down at Kidd. "And you, too, Kidd."

Twoey and Kidd looked at each other as if they had just been given the best present in the world.

CHAPTER TWENTY–SIX

Life After Racing

After Twoey and Kidd were loaded into the woman's horse trailer, Twoey looked out the window at the racetrack. An unexpected sadness came over him when he realized he would never again be on a racetrack. He would never experience all the familiar sounds and smells. He would never race again. Racing had been his life. It had been the only life he had known.

As he watched, the van pulled away and the racetrack began to disappear. The life he had known was gone forever. It had been a good life though—one he had enjoyed and excelled in.

Twoey hadn't thought of the past for a long time. It made him too sad. But now he allowed himself to remember some of the happier times in his racing career. He remembered how it felt to sprint out of the gate and run as fast as he could, staying on the rail. He could remember the feeling of flying on the wind.

Twoey smiled when he thought of the royal treatment he had been given when he entered the winner's circle. He could almost feel the heat from the flashbulbs as picture after picture was taken.

He even thought of his training on the treadmill, when he had to run for miles to increase his endurance. He admitted to himself, he had enjoyed it all. He was pleased that remembering the past now comforted him. His heart felt full of hope.

Twoey looked down at his buddy and was happy to see that Kidd felt as relaxed and confident as he did. Kidd was curled up, sound asleep.

* * * *

Twoey wasn't taken to a farm as he had expected, but rather to a hospital for horses.

"We need to get some x-rays of that leg, Twoey," the veterinarian explained. "You may need some surgery to repair the injury. Kidd can stay here, too, while you're evaluated."

The doctors at Michigan State University Veterinary Teaching Hospital had worked with CANTER-owned thoroughbreds for several years, performing surgeries to give injured thoroughbreds a chance to live a pain-free life.

Dr. John Stick, Chief of Staff of the Large Animal Hospital, greeted Twoey. "You're a fine looking fellow," he said to Twoey as he checked him over. "Let's see if we can get that leg fixed up."

Later that day, the diagnosis was given to Twoey's rescuers. "It's not good. The x-rays indicate that he's been given so many cortisone shots that the leg bone has holes in it. He also has so many old bone chips in his knees that we can't remove them through surgery. I'm sorry but we can't do anything for him. He should never be ridden again."

The vet looked at Twoey and then gave the teary-eyed CANTER volunteers some hope. "I know, in some cases like this, it might be better to give up on a horse with so many injuries, but Twoey has a terrific attitude. He has that wonderful thoroughbred heart that makes him overcome any obstacle."

Dr. Stick patted Twoey's head. "He needs a home where

he will be loved and given lots of attention. He's earned it. His working days are over.

As the CANTER volunteers led Twoey and Kidd to the horse van, they were worried about Twoey's future. It would be difficult to find a buyer for a thoroughbred that could not even be ridden on a trail. Most of the rescued horses were sold to owners who wanted to retrain them as show horses.

The rescuers knew the success stories by heart and there were many. Most former thoroughbred racehorses were now winning competitions in jumping, dressage, and eventing. But that would not be Twoey's future. For now, he would live at a CANTER foster horse farm until it could be decided what to do with him...and with Kidd.

Twoey sensed disappointment and anxiety. He suddenly was not as confident about his future as he had been when he arrived at the hospital. His other hospital experience in California had been a good one and he became healthy again. He was surprisingly disappointed that he would not be treated at this hospital.

Kidd felt the change in Twoey's attitude. They had gone into the hospital full of hope and anticipation. Now, Kidd saw that the hope had left Twoey's eyes.

Twoey knew the nice people were trying to help him, but he was afraid that maybe no one could help him. The hope Twoey had felt hours earlier was replaced by fear.

* * * *

At his foster home, Twoey was afraid to trust anyone. His fear kept him from being friendly. Kidd protected Twoey as much as he could. He slept at the stall gate and let out a loud threatening noise whenever anyone came near.

When food was brought to their stall, Twoey would kick

and threaten to bite, encouraging everyone to leave him alone. And they did.

Although they were afraid to trust humans, Twoey and Kidd were lonely without human attention.

* * * *

When a little boy and two little girls came up to their stall door and looked inside, Twoey slowly moved closer to the door. The children moved back a little because they had been told that the horse might bite. Twoey saw that they were afraid of him and he felt ashamed of his mean reputation. He softly whinnied as if asking them to come closer. They did.

"We brought you carrots," the little boy said. "We heard you like them.

Twoey nodded his head as if to say "yes" and the children laughed as they handed him a carrot. While Twoey was enjoying his treat, the children stooped down to see Kidd up close.

Kidd also was lonely for affection. He timidly moved closer to the children. They handed Kidd a carrot and giggled when he ate it as fast as he could.

"See you later," they yelled as they skipped away from the stall door.

"It was wrong of me to act so mean just because I was afraid and wanted to scare everyone away from us," Twoey admitted. "I'm sorry, Kidd."

"It's okay. I was afraid, too, but being afraid isn't nearly as satisfying as being happy," Kidd said. "Let's not ever be afraid again, Twoey." Twoey agreed with his friend.

* * * *

The children, Kayla, Leah, and Cody, came often to visit Twoey and Kidd. They began leading them out to the pasture where they would brush Twoey. Twoey relaxed and enjoyed the attention. It felt so good to be cared for and groomed again.

He was even getting some exercise. He carefully walked around the pasture and strengthened his leg, stopping when it started hurting too badly. While Twoey completed his circle around the pasture, Kidd found a soft pillow of grass and went to sleep.

Twoey made the children laugh whenever he nuzzled their heads, necks, backs, and arms. They thought he was looking for carrot treats, and he enjoyed hearing their laughter. It reminded Twoey of Amy and how she had laughed when he grabbed the back of her jacket. He often thought of Amy—many happy memories. When the memories became sad, he tried to think of something else.

Often alone in the pasture, Twoey and Kidd would take advantage of the soft grass and warm sun to stretch out and take a nap. They were very happy again.

* * * *

One day the children and their parents came to talk to Twoey and Kidd. They were stroking Twoey's neck while explaining that Twoey and Kidd were being taken to another home.

Twoey felt the fear begin inside him, and he tried to overcome it. He saw that the children were not crying. They were happy for him as they described where he would live. He pushed the fear to the back of his mind.

"You'll never have to move again," Leah proudly told Twoey.

"And you and Kidd will always be together," Cody quickly added.

"You've worked hard all your life, Twoey," their mother

told him, as she kept stroking his neck. "You deserve to relax and not work anymore."

"You'll love this new place!" Kayla exclaimed with excitement, "Lots of green pastures and you can do whatever you want."

"And they'll give you lots of carrots," Cody promised.

Twoey and Kidd soon found themselves riding again in a horse van to yet another new home. Despite the reassurances of the children that they would love this place, Twoey held back any enthusiasm, any hope. He did not want to be disappointed again. He decided that he had better enjoy the ride because, if Leah was right, this might be the last time he would ride in a van to a new home.

Twoey looked out to see the changing scenery. He let the air blow over him, enjoying the feeling. The sky was a bright, sunny blue. Twoey thought it was a good sign. The hope began to return to his heart. He looked forward to seeing his new, maybe his last, home.

CHAPTER TWENTY-SEVEN

Finding the Winner's Circle

The first thing Twoey saw when the horse van stopped was a sign that read "Thoroughbred Retirement Farm." Behind it were new, well-kept barns and grassy pastures as far as he could see.

Kidd stretched, waking up from his nap that had lasted the whole trip. "Are we there yet?" he asked Twoey.

"We have arrived," Twoey answered with finality. He felt that the word meant more than just arriving at a new farm. He and Kidd had come home. Twoey believed they had finally "arrived" at the time in their lives when they no longer had to worry about anything. They had "arrived" to find happiness, contentment, and pleasure. Twoey felt more than hope. He just knew in his heart there were people here who would love them and take care of them.

When Twoey and Kidd were led out of the van, Twoey could not believe what he was seeing. For a moment he thought he was dreaming. He shook his head to make sure he was awake and when he looked again, she was still there—his beloved Amy.

"Twoey!" Amy cried out as tears streamed down her face. "Thank goodness you're here safely." She couldn't say any more. She just wanted to hug him and hold onto him to make sure he was real.

Kidd couldn't believe it was really Amy. Kidd snuggled next to her legs giving her his goat hug. She bent over to pat his head.

"Kidd, you did a good job watching over Twoey, thanks." Amy couldn't stop hugging Twoey. She never wanted to let go of him again. They had been separated for years. That's in the past, she thought, we'll always be together now. I can hug Twoey every day. Her someday was today.

"C'mon. I'll show you around your new home," Amy told Twoey and Kidd. "I live here, too. I'm going to vet school and I volunteered to live and work at the Thoroughbred Retirement Farm," Amy explained.

Then she looked at Twoey, knowing the pain and suffering he had endured. Sadly she said, "I looked all over for you, Twoey. Just about the time I caught up with one of your owners, I was told you had been sold to someone else, then someone else."

"When your birthday carrot cake was returned with a stamp that read 'address unknown,' I cried, feeling that I had let you down." Her tears continued.

Twoey nuzzled her neck, trying to tell her he had missed her.

"You always understood everything I tried to tell you," Amy said, smiling through her tears. Twoey nodded, as he had done as a young colt, to let her know he agreed with her.

She laughed. "You always did agree with me." She looked warmly into his eyes and said, "Thank goodness I found you! I couldn't believe it when I read on the Internet that the thoroughbred rescue group, CANTER, had gotten you off the racetrack."

Amy's eyes filled with tears again as she said, "They saved you, Twoey. And they saved Kidd, too. I don't want to think what might have happened to you." Twoey gave Amy another nuzzle to make her smile.

"From the minute you were born, I knew you were a survivor," Amy told him. "You've learned how to forget the bad things in your past and look to the future with hope. Now there's no more looking back."

Twoey felt so happy, he started prancing to let Amy know.

As Amy led her favorite thoroughbred and his best friend to their new home, they walked by a pasture. Twoey saw thoroughbreds grazing and resting and playing. He let out a big sigh. He thought to himself that he was finally home.

Kidd was looking at the pasture, too, but he didn't see the thoroughbreds. The prettiest goat he had ever seen was staring at him through the fence.

"Hi," she said to Kidd, in a soft voice. "My name is Reindeer. What's yours?"

Kidd couldn't seem to get his voice to work. He finally managed to say, "I'm Captain Kidd."

Reindeer blinked her big eyes at Kidd and said, "I'll see you around Captain Kidd."

"Yeah, sure," Kidd shyly answered back, not knowing what to say. His heart was pounding. He caught up to Twoey and Amy but kept glancing back to see if Reindeer was watching him. She was.

* * * *

Twoey was sure that this place was heaven for horses. Everyday he was allowed to graze in the pasture, sleep, or play with the other horses. Everyday he saw Amy.

Kidd saw his goat friend, Reindeer, every day and they would take off running all over the farm. He'd check on Twoey about three times a day, but after deciding Twoey was just fine, he and Reindeer would run off again.

Twoey watched Kidd and Reindeer as they frolicked around the farm, going on daily adventures—adventures he and Kidd used to share.

Amy was walking up to Twoey when she noticed how he held his head down and seemed to be sad. She knew her surprise would cheer him up. She began brushing and grooming him. "We've got to get you looking your best. You have a visitor coming this afternoon," she explained.

Twoey always felt better when his coat was clean and gleaming. He wondered if Mr. Brand was coming, or maybe Louie. He loved surprises, but only good ones.

Twoey had been lying in the sun in the pasture and thought he must have fallen asleep. Or was he still sleeping? The vision he saw was so beautiful that he believed he must be dreaming.

"Hi, Twoey." The voice was soft and silky.

Twoey didn't speak. He was thinking—dreams don't speak so clearly, do they? "Am I dreaming?" he finally asked the vision.

"No, you're not," the vision answered. "It's me, Angel Eyes. It's been so long since you've seen me, I wasn't sure you'd recognize me."

Twoey was instantly awake and on his feet, not believing she was really here with him. "I have never forgotten you, Angel," Twoey said, as he came closer to nuzzle her neck.

Twoey kept rubbing his neck against Angel's neck, reassuring himself that she was real. Angel didn't move away, but returned the nuzzle.

After a while, Angel suggested they move under the shade of a tree. She listened as Twoey relived his racing career, cheering with him as he won the big races and crying with him as he fell in pain.

Twoey was fascinated by Angel's stories of performing

exact routines in the show ring and jumping hurdles while following a set path around the arena.

Despite their lives while apart, it seemed to Twoey as if they had actually always been together. Twoey felt so warm inside, he thought his heart might melt. He realized she had kept him in her heart, just as he had placed her in his heart.

The sun was beginning to set. Twoey began to feel afraid that he and Angel would be separated again.

"I want you to stay here with me," Twoey pleaded.

Angel Eyes smiled. "I'm not going anywhere else, Twoey."

Amy was walking toward Twoey and Angel Eyes, with Captain Kidd and Reindeer at her heels. Twoey watched them. He suddenly understood what it truly meant to be a champion.

Twoey had always thought that his perfect world was on the racetrack and in the winner's circle. Now he realized that he was surrounded by those who loved him—Angel, Kidd, Amy—and the loving memories of his mom, Diamond Knight, and Louie. It was a circle of love. A winner's circle that he would never have to leave again.

The End

The Real Story of
Twoey and Kidd the Goat

Twoey is a real thoroughbred racehorse. His registered name is Two Links Back, but he was nicknamed Twoey when he was just a foal. At 16.3 hands tall, he is also called the gentle giant because of his size and love of attention. As you'll see from his picture on the jacket, he is a dark bay, almost black, color with a small white star on his forehead. He is descended from the champion racehorse Nasrullah.

Kidd the goat was also a real goat and was Twoey's best friend. During Twoey's six-year racing career, Kidd would go with Twoey to the starting gate at racetracks and he would stay with Twoey in his stall.

Two Links Back (Twoey) was named 1995 Colt of the Year when he raced as a three year old in Illinois. He retired to a thoroughbred retirement farm in Missouri, with his best friend Kidd, in 2001. His last race was in the fall of 2000 at the age of eight.

The thoroughbred placement organization, CANTER (Communication Alliance to Network Thoroughbred Ex-Racehorses), purchased Twoey for $600 from his owner at Great Lakes Downs in Muskegon, Michigan, in November 2000. Since he had always been Twoey's constant companion, Kidd the goat came with Twoey.

Through donations to CANTER, Michigan State University's Veterinary Teaching Hospital performs surgeries on injured CANTER thoroughbreds, enabling them to succeed in new careers such as dressage, jumping, and eventing. MSU equine veterinary students experience unique medical training by assisting with x-rays, diagnosis, surgery, medical treatment, and follow up. CANTER thoroughbreds are rehabilitated and receive training at boarding facilities. When ready, the horse is listed for sale on CANTER's web site to an approved non-racing home.

Because Twoey could never be ridden again, CANTER volunteers had difficulty finding a buyer. Instead, volunteers found a retirement home filled with green pastures for Twoey and Kidd.

EXCERPTS FROM TWOEY'S CAREGIVER AT THE RETIREMENT HOME

After Twoey and Kidd had arrived at the thoroughbred retirement farm in Missouri, their caretaker Robin Hurst wrote on January 31, 2001:

Just a short note to tell you that the new arrivals, the goat and his horse, are safe and happily settling in. The two of them are a hoot and the goat reminds me of a troll under a bridge, as he stands under the belly of this giant of a horse. We love them to pieces and they are a joy.

On February 6, 2001, Robin writes:

It is our pleasure to have the dynamic duo on our premises. It appears both bachelors have developed new love interests. First, the Kidd had an admirer from the moment he stepped on the place. Her name is Reindeer and she is an ancient female LaMoncha-Angora cross goat that we rescued last spring. She is super sweet and never quite bonded with our five other goats and two pot-bellied pigs. She took one look at the Kidd and fell instantly in love.

The Kidd and Twoey were originally placed in an adjacent pasture to Reindeer. She spent the first three days of their arrival plastered to the fence, crying out to the Kidd. He ignored her. It was pitiful.

Then, about the fourth day, I went outside to do the morning feeding and Reindeer had squeezed through the gate and had joined Kidd and Twoey. It was the cutest thing I had ever seen because as I called the Kidd and Twoey up for breakfast, they had a third member running behind them.

At first Kidd was torn with his loyalty to Twoey. Now, however, it seems that Twoey has a love interest of his own. Her name is Rainy Summer and she is a retired racetrack thoroughbred mare. They struck up a relationship over the fence and now Rainy and Twoey eat in separate buckets, but next to one another, and the Kidd and Reindeer eat in the same flat pan (followed by much grooming afterwards).

They are all too cute.

On May 13, 2001, Robin writes:

Twoey has made a remarkable transition to his new laid-back life of eating, drinking, snacking, and sleeping. He is much, much calmer. He is my absolute favorite because he is such a contrast of different lives. I dearly love this gentle being.

The Kidd rotates himself (slinks under whatever fence his belly does not get caught in) from herd to herd, but *mostly he stays near Twoey. The Kidd always takes upon himself to try and nurse the needy and my newest mare is his latest venture.*

His and Twoey's relationship has changed into being less neurotic. Twoey is not obsessed with the Kidd's whereabouts every minute and as long as the Kidd checks in with him a couple of times a day, Twoey is cool with it.

Twoey is an incredible horse of love and affection.

A FINAL NOTE

Two Links Back (Twoey) still lives happily at the thoroughbred retirement home in Missouri. Kidd the goat died peacefully there after living out the rest of his life with his best friend, Twoey.

To find out more about CANTER's work rescuing thoroughbreds, visit their web site www.canterusa.org.

To learn more about the Veterinary Teaching Hospital at Michigan State University visit www.cvm.msu.edu.